Embracing Her Inheritance

CROSSRIVER BOOKS BY DEBRA L. BUTTERFIELD

HER INHERITANCE SERIES

Claiming Her Inheritance
Discovering Her Inheritance
Embracing Her Inheritance

OTHER FICTION

Mystery on Maple Hill, a short story

NONFICTION

Self-editing & Publishing Tips for Indie Authors
7 Cheat Sheets to Cut Editing Costs
Unshakable Faith, a Bible study
Unshakable Faith Leaders Guide
Carried by Grace: a guide for mothers of victims of sexual abuse

COMPILED AND EDITED

Abba's Promise: 33 Stories of God's Pledge to Provide
Abba's Answers: 30 Stories of God's Answers to Prayer

Embracing Her Inheritance

DEBRA L. BUTTERFIELD

ST. JOSEPH, MISSOURI USA

EMBRACING HER INHERITANCE
Copyright © 2024 Debra L. Butterfield

ISBN: 978-1-936501-92-2

Scripture quotations are taken from the Holy Bible, New Living Translation, copyright ©1996, 2004, 2007, 2013 by Tyndale House Foundation. Used by permission of Tyndale House Publishers, Inc., Carol Stream, Illinois 60188. All rights reserved.

Scripture taken from the New King James Version®. Copyright © 1982 by Thomas Nelson. Used by permission. All rights reserved.

For more information on Debra L. Butterfield, visit DebraLButterfield.com

Cover Art: iStock.com/Debi Bishop
Cover Design: Debra L. Butterfield

Printed in the United States of America.

Prologue

*C*hronicle reporter Elizabeth Travers stared at the fire station. The bright morning sun only served to accentuate her frustration with mundane assignments. Interviewing the fire chief sounded as thrilling as the latest agricultural workshop on insect and weed management, but maybe she'd get a front page story out of it instead of three lines next to the want-ad section. She was going to make it to a regional TV station this year even if she had to lie, cheat, or sleep her way there.

A fireman met her as she entered the station. "Can I help you?" he asked.

"Yes. I'm here from the *Chronicle* to interview Chief Schmidt."

"That's me. Let's go to my office. Would you like some coffee?"

"No thank you." No station house sludge for her. "We'd like to do a story on the recent blizzard and how it impacted the area. How did you and your men cope with conditions? Were there more calls than normal?" She followed Chief Schmidt as he made his way to his office.

"Actually, thank the good Lord, we had very few calls. But we did have one extraordinary call out down near Ardmore." The chief stopped and turned to face her. "I'll never forget what we found once we got there."

The chief stared at her for several agonizing moments as if searching her soul. She imagined a grizzly scene of frozen bodies trapped in a car, but his tone was positive and excited. "What did you find?"

"A miracle, Miss Travers…We found a miracle."

Chapter One
SALLY

"May integrity and honesty protect me, for I
put my hope in you." Psalm 25:21

ately, my life has been one bombshell after another.

I inherited an annual six-figure income from a total stranger, Chase Reynolds, Jr. Discovered I had an identical twin sister, Abby Reynolds. Was bitten by a rattlesnake, arrested for theft and jailed, then bailed out but nearly murdered. Six weeks later my father died. And let's not forget, I learned Abby and I have a brother. I felt like I was back in the Marine Corps fighting in the Middle East. All this carried the emotional impact of an IED.

A long weekend of being stranded with Abby and three strangers in a little country church by a blizzard merely added to my burgeoning list. Life was never this exciting back home in Kansas City.

God had turned my life upside down, and even after two days of lounging in a hotel room in Scottsbluff, Nebraska, I was no closer to grasping the message He was trying to send me. Maybe it would all make sense when we found our brother.

"Let's go grab some lunch." Abby slapped shut the book she was reading, bringing my attention to the here and now.

"I'll second that idea. Let's talk strategy on finding our brother." We slipped on our coats, grabbed our purses, and walked across the street to Hungry Man's Diner.

Sarah, my friend from high school who waitressed at the diner, greeted us with a cheerful, "Hi, Sally, hi, Abby. Take a seat anywhere. You want your usual coffee and tea?"

"Yes," Abby and I chimed.

I selected a table that offered the best view of the diner's TV. I wanted to catch some of the news. Before grabbing a menu, I glanced at the special-of-the-day listed on the board near the cash register. Chicken strips with fries and a cup of soup caught my interest. We took our seats and I turned my attention to the news.

"… in Ardmore with Edgemont *Chronicle* reporter Elizabeth Travers. Elizabeth, thank you for bringing this story to our attention. What have you found?"

A slender brunette woman appeared on the screen. Her shoulder-length hair blew wildly across her face despite the knitted hat pulled down over her ears.

"Abby, look!" I pointed to the TV. The reporter stood in front of the church we'd been stranded at.

"Michael, I spoke with Edgemont fire chief Warren Schmidt yesterday. He and his men responded to a head injury call due to a car accident here at Christ Community Church five miles north of Ardmore, South Dakota, in the very early hours of Monday morning. It took them four hours to traverse the twenty-two miles from Edgemont to Ardmore due to the blizzard conditions." She spoke with the overly enthusiastic voice so common to reporters.

The camera panned the landscape. Despite the last two days of warmer temps, the area still looked like the Antarctic tundra we had experienced.

I spotted Sarah in my peripheral vision, her pad and pencil poised to take our order. "Give me a minute, Sarah. I want to catch this news." I pointed toward the TV, keeping my eyes riveted on the screen.

"Four people were stranded here from last Friday until Monday, along with the pastor of the church, Reverend Joshua Salem." Travers pulled a strand of hair away from her mouth, and the expression on her face turned to one of doubt and surprise. "But there's a bizarre twist to this incident. The church shut down in May 1992 due to a fire and Reverend Salem, though not injured by the fire, died one month later. But there's more. First, let's take a look inside."

She walked up the steps to the front door that banged against a metal box used to prop it open. The cameraman followed closely behind. The stairs and landing were again covered in snow—we had shoveled it—but a new much smaller path for the reporter had apparently been cleared.

Now the camera panned the sanctuary, showing the burned half of the church and four boarded windows. Dead leaves and snow dusted the floor.

"How are these people faring now, Elizabeth? How did the fire department effect rescue?" the news anchor asked.

"That's the amazing part, Michael. Chief Schmidt said what occurred here was nothing short of a miracle. The man claiming to be Reverend Salem—"

"Claiming?" Abby said over the reporter.

"—greeted the chief and his men and fed them pancakes, eggs, bacon, and hot coffee. The sanctuary was clean and warm. Everyone was quite well."

"How could any of that be possible in such a derelict building?" the anchor responded. "And the person with the head injury?"

"She stated Jesus had healed her, if you can believe that." Sarcasm tinged the reporter's voice. She frowned and lifted her eyebrows. "The paramedics thoroughly examined her and found her in good health. The police and a wrecker were dispatched to help them get back on the road as soon as highway maintenance had it cleared. As I observe this crumbling building, I can't help but wonder if the events that took place here this past weekend were a genuine miracle, as Chief Schmidt reported, or nothing but an elaborate hoax."

"We look forward to hearing more as you investigate further," the anchorman said. "Thank you, Elizabeth. And now a look at today's weather."

"What's got you so interested in this report, Sally?" Sarah asked. Apparently she watched it while waiting for our order.

9

"Because she's talking about us."

"What? How horrible. That must have been awful."

"That's just the thing, Sarah. It wasn't. The church didn't look at all like what we saw on the news just now," I said.

"Exactly," Abby agreed. "No boarded windows, plenty of warmth from the wood-burning pot belly stove, and all the food we needed."

"There was even electricity when we first arrived, but the storm knocked it out later that day. They're saying it was a hoax." I dropped back in my chair and looked at Abby. "How can they possibly think four total strangers staged a hoax in the middle of a blizzard…and that any one of us would know the reverend who pastored that church?"

"Well, Sally," Sarah said, "you'll just have to set them straight."

Certainly not a task I wanted to add to my to-do list. My opinion of the media was so low you'd have to pull it up out of the gutter. *Setting them straight* struck me as impossible. I cringed. Was this yet another bombshell about to explode in my life?

Talking strategy about how to find our brother melted like the snow outside. Instead, we spent our lunch discussing how or even whether to respond to the reporter's claims, without coming to any conclusion.

Chapter Two
CHASE

"Tune your ears to wisdom, and concentrate
on understanding." Proverbs 2:2

I was standing at the check-in desk when Sally and Abby entered the hotel lobby. My two suitcases sat at my feet. I had just flown in from Great Falls, Montana, and hoped to get settled into my room before stepping into the boxing ring with the petite spitfire Sally Clark.

"Chase! What a surprise. What are you doing here?" Abby hugged me.

I noted the surprise on Sally's face, then turned to my sister—oops, my adopted sister—Abby. I would never get used to calling her that, not after fifty-eight years of only knowing her as my sister. Not the wisest decision my parents ever made not to tell us Abby was adopted. "I came to update you with what Karl found out about the orphanage you were in and to help you two with the search for your orphaned brother. I was just checking in." I turned back to the hotel clerk who handed me the key card to my room. I pocketed the card, then picked up my suitcases. "You both look good. Radiant, in fact. Why don't you join me in my room. You can tell me all about your weekend being stranded and then I'll fill you in on what Karl found."

They followed me down the first-floor hallway to my room and made themselves comfortable at the table while I stashed my suitcases, tossed my Stetson on the bed, and hung my coat. Given how much Sally protested last week when I showed up uninvited to her father's funeral, I didn't know quite what to think about her lack of protest at my presence now.

"So how are you two doing after your ordeal? All caught up on your sleep?" I took a seat at the table.

"I wouldn't call it an ordeal by any means," Abby said. "And yes, we've been doing nothing but relaxing for the last two days."

"So give me the full story." I leaned forward on the table.

"Wait, Chase."

Sally put her hand on my forearm, putting a stop to my words.

"I need to apologize first."

"For what?"

"For my rudeness last week. You came here to Scottsbluff to my father's funeral to show your support, and all I did was grouch at you. And now here you are to help without even being asked. I'm sorry."

"Apology accepted. Sounds like your time being stranded has… what words am I looking for?…softened your heart?"

Sally scoffed and fidgeted in her chair. "That's an understatement. When you hear the whole story, you'll be amazed. It's already made the news—"

"Made the news? When?" I sat up.

"We saw a report while we were at lunch just now. They're asking was it a miracle or a hoax." Sally crossed her arms and clenched her jaw.

"A hoax? Hmmm. I want the full story."

Sally pulled her phone from her back pants pocket and started a recording app.

"You're recording this?" I looked at her, frowning.

She tilted her head at me and smirked. Glee shone in her eyes. "This way we don't have to tell the story a hundred times. Those who want to know can listen to the recording. You start, Abby."

"Like I told you when we spoke Monday, Reverend Salem welcomed us to the church. I guessed his age in the thirties. Do you agree, Sally?"

"Yeah, I'd say that's accurate."

"Initially the building had electricity," Abby continued, "but the storm made quick work of that. A pot belly stove kept us warm, and we cooked all our meals there. The place looked like something out of the 1940s, but we lacked nothing…aside from having beds to sleep on."

"But the pews did have cushions about three or four inches thick. If not for that, sleeping on the floor would have been more comfortable," Sally interjected. "The age of the place was very apparent in the kitchen. The General Electric refrigerator definitely said 1940s. You know, the kind that had a small freezer section inside the refrigerator instead of entirely separate. And no stove. I thought that was especially odd. When Cohen arrived, he insisted the pot belly was stone cold. He touched it twice and never burned his hand." Sally shook her head as she spoke, her eyes wide. "It shocked me because I had coffee brewing and heard it bubbling. When I poured steaming coffee into his cup, it astonished him. Literally knocked him off his feet."

"He saw the place so differently that first day there," Abby continued. "Boarded windows, burned pews, no heat, no food. But in the end, he saw it just as we did, right down to the stained-glass window behind the pulpit. He and his daughter, Hannah, crashed into the ditch near the church. That's how they ended up there. Both of them were healed of the minor injuries they got in the crash."

"That stained-glass window has me wondering. In the news report we saw thirty minutes ago, there wasn't one. Only a solid wall behind the pulpit." Sally looked at Abby. "Any thoughts on that?"

"Not at the moment. That window transfixed Hannah. I wonder if she took a picture of it."

"We definitely need to ask." Sally nodded, her torso rocking in response.

"What else happened?" I listened attentively as they each explained their perspective of the miracle that occurred at Christ Community Church while stranded by a blizzard. Vibrancy resounded in Sally's words. Delight emanated from her face. I sensed a peace from her that hadn't been there twelve weeks ago when she came to my Montana cattle ranch to claim her inheritance from Pop.

"Turns out we all had the same dream," Sally paused, "no, it had to be a vision."

"Wait a minute. You all had the same vision?"

"Yes," Abby confirmed. "We only figured that out because Cohen heard Sally telling me about her strange dream."

"We were at Capernaum with Jesus when he healed the paralytic let down through the roof. He healed Cohen's daughter, Hannah. She bumped her head on the car window when they crashed into the ditch. She was fine that first day, but the next day she had a headache and got really sick as the day progressed. Dream, vision, however you want to describe it, it happened for real. Hannah was completely well the next morning."

"Wow," was the only word I could find to respond with.

Sally briefly closed her eyes and sighed deeply, then fixed her gaze on me. "The love that beamed from Jesus' eyes. He said two words to me. *Let go.*"

"Of what?" I asked.

"The anger I unconsciously functioned from. Jesus helped me let go of it. That and the pain associated with the childhood events that provoked my anger."

"This certainly explains the radiance you each have…Wow, again. It must have been amazing to be in Jesus' presence in a physical way. I'm thrilled for you both." I dropped back in my chair, stunned. "And according to the policeman there'd been a fire at the church in 1992 and Reverend Salem died thirty days after that?"

"You got it." Abby nodded.

"I'm not surprised it made the news…or at their reaction." I leaned forward and put my elbows on the table, ready to hear more, but Sally stopped the recording app and pocketed her phone.

"I'm not sure I want reporters and TV cameras descending on me. Abby and I discussed whether to attempt a response to the TV news channel but didn't come to any decision. How did they even find out about it? I doubt Cohen said anything. Maybe the policeman or the crew from the fire station up in Edgemont? Surely they wouldn't blab about their call outs."

"Edgemont?" Chase asked.

"Sorry. Edgemont, South Dakota. That was the nearest town with a 911 response team," Sally explained.

"The reporter said she talked with the fire chief. I expect she went looking for news of how the blizzard impacted people." Abby pulled a pen and a small notebook from her purse. "Now it's our turn."

"Sally, our lawyer is very thorough in everything he does, but Karl still wonders why he didn't find this information during his initial research on you all those years ago when Mom and Pop first met you in Paris. Obviously the Lord's hand is in this. Karl's father handled Abby's adoption and the records revealed her parents died in a car accident, but not who her parents were. Nor had he been able to find anything that connected you two. Yesterday morning he called with the news he'd found the record of your arrival—you two and your brother—at the Lowenfeld orphanage. The police were unable to find any known relatives."

Sally sat up straight, her Montana-sky-blue eyes sparkled like the sun. "If he found that, then he discovered who our parents were as well."

"He did. George and Christine Leonard. Your brother's name is Robert."

"Chase, that's wonderful," Sally blurted and grabbed Abby's hand. "That should help tremendously in finding him. Was Karl able to find any adoption records on him?"

"I didn't ask him that. I could see if his office has time to take it on."

"That's a thought. Lawyers certainly know all the channels and how to open the doors." Sally released Abby's hand and shrugged. "What do you think, Abby?"

"Since the adoption took place here in Nebraska, why don't you have Mr. Brown do it? He'd be familiar with the Nebraska laws that govern such a search."

"Remind me. Who's Mr. Brown?" I said.

"The lawyer who's handling my father's estate." Sally pulled her phone out of her back pants pocket again. "I'll call his office right now and see if he has time open yet this week to see me."

While Sally made the phone call, I watched Abby. The distant look in her eyes told me she was somewhere far from the current conversation. "Abby, you seem lost in thought."

"I was wondering how Cohen and Hannah were doing."

"Tell me about them, starting with their full name."

"Cohen and Hannah Reed. Don't know much. He's a business consultant here in Scottsbluff. Divorced. Hannah attends college nearby. She's such a sweet girl."

I looked at Sally who wiggled her eyebrows then slightly tipped her body toward Abby. Was she trying to tell me something?

Abby's text message alert dinged.

"Excuse me." Abby reached down to her purse on the floor and dug out her phone.

"Did Mr. Brown have an opening?" I asked Sally.

"Yes, I'm set for Friday at nine."

"Do you mind if I join you?" Was I asking too much?

"No, I don't mind. Abby do you want to come?"

"No, I don't see the need." She continued texting.

"Well, Sally, seems my father's death set off quite a cascade of dominoes in your life. Any plans for tomorrow?"

"My father had everything put into storage when he was sent to prison. His executor is sorting through it tomorrow and invited me to join him. Thought there might be items I'd like to keep. We could use your muscles. You game?" Sally asked.

"I'm here to help in any way I can. You don't think going through your father's things will be too painful? Dredge up too many awful memories?"

She shrugged. "It might bring up memories, but like I said, Jesus washed away the pain during my last night at the church."

Abby finished typing a text message and put her phone on the table. "Sally, while you and Chase do that, I think I'll go to the library and search the archives for car accidents. Maybe I can learn more about our parents."

"Why do I feel like I'm in the middle of an adventure story?" Sally asked.

"Because you are," I said.

"Really?"

"Yes!" Abby grinned, her eyes bright. "Walking with God is always an adventure."

16

Abby's phone dinged with another text message. She glanced at it.

"Something pressing?" I asked.

"Cohen's asked me to dinner on Friday. I'd like to say yes. You and Sally can keep yourselves busy, right?"

"Of course we can." Sally smiled and gave me a firm nod.

Was a relationship budding between Abby and Cohen?

Chapter Three

SALLY

"Stop being angry! Turn from your rage! Do not lose
your temper—it only leads to harm." Psalm 37:8

Thursday morning, first thing after breakfast at the hotel buffet, Chase Reynolds III and I took my car and drove to the storage unit. Abby took Chase's rental car and headed to the library. When we arrived at the storage unit, Jeremiah Nathaniel, my father's executor, and his grandson were already there and had pulled out several smaller pieces of furniture.

The blizzard hadn't dumped as much snow on Scottsbluff as it had farther north in South Dakota, but large piles of snow occupied the far corners of the lot. The pavement in front of the unit was clear and dry, thank goodness.

"Good morning, Jeremiah. Hard at work, I see. Are we late? I thought you told me nine o' clock."

"You're right on time. My grandson here showed up at my place at 8:30, rarin' to go, so we did."

I reached my hand out to his grandson. I figured him to be about twenty-five. He looked a lot like his grandfather, though much younger and slimmer.

"I'm Aaron. Nice to meet you."

"I'm Sally Clark. This is Chase Reynolds." I pointed to Chase standing beside me.

"Great Stetson you've got." Aaron shook Chase's hand.

"Thank you." Chase turned and shook Jeremiah's hand. "Nice of you to give Sally the option of keeping some things."

"Where do we start?" I held out my arms, my hands palms up.

"I've arranged for a sale right here tomorrow at one," Jeremiah began. "It's mostly furniture, but there's about ten boxes at the back of the unit you'll want to go through. I reckon we can get through it all today."

Chase and Aaron hauled out the remaining furniture, and Jeremiah and I cleaned, dusted, and wiped away cobwebs. Before long, I unzipped my jacket and pulled off my gloves. The temperature rose quickly as the sun traveled its circuit, and the piles of snow in the corners of the lot grew considerably smaller. Three hours later, that task was done. Would it go back in as easily as it had come out?

"Aaron, I think they sell bottled water at the office." Jeremiah handed him several bills. "Go grab us each a bottle and we'll take a short break."

Chuckling, I took a seat on the couch to await Aaron's return.

"What's so funny?" Chase sat beside me.

"Sitting on a couch, outside, in the middle of...storage units." I zipped my jacket again.

"Yeah, that is a bit odd." Chase smiled.

"Jeremiah, do you have any idea what's in those boxes?" I pointed to the boxes at the back of the ten-by-thirty foot unit.

"Usual stuff. Clothes, dishes, some books maybe. It's been too long since I packed it all. It'll sell as is, the whole box. This place has sales regular-like for units that have been abandoned. That's how they recoup their losses."

"Smart. Have you advertised your sale?" Chase asked.

"There's a flyer in the storage unit office and I've had an ad in the paper for several days. I'll probably donate what doesn't sell to Goodwill. Do you want any of this furniture, Sally?"

"Maybe that cedar chest, but I don't need the blankets that are in it." Aaron returned with the bottles of water.

"Thanks, Aaron." I took a long swig. Admittedly, I would have liked a cup of hot chocolate, but I was grateful for the water too. "I'd better get back at it." I stuffed my water into my jacket pocket and headed to the boxes.

"How can I help with these?" Chase stood behind me.

"Pull down the boxes that are stacked. Then make sure what's in the box is what it says. Maybe root through it a bit to ensure something different isn't buried at the bottom."

Chase lifted the first box from the stack and carried it closer to the door for more light. While he brought boxes to the door, I dusted off the top then started digging through them. I found exactly what Jeremiah said. Dishes, clothes, bed linens, though I hadn't spotted any books yet—a few dead bugs but thankfully no dead mice or rats. My morning of dusting the furniture left my sinuses congested, effectively blocking any potential disagreeable odors that might have assaulted my nose.

Then I got to a dish box marked *Helen's things.*

I froze, staring at those words. A small cannonball hit me in the pit of my stomach. Helen was my adoptive mom. I thought my adoptive father had gotten rid of all her stuff. But given he'd gone off the deep end when she died, I shouldn't have been surprised he kept things of hers he might cherish. I hesitated to open the box.

"Something wrong?" Chase's question startled me. He stood beside me, his bottle of water in hand. His six-foot-plus height and the bulk of his solid muscles gave me the impression of standing next to a brick wall. His warmth diffused my chill. Ranching certainly kept him fit. His rugged presence reassured me.

"No, I...this box ambushed me."

"Who's Helen?"

"My adoptive mom. I didn't know my father kept any of her things. Guess I'd better look inside, but I'm..."

"Want me to do it?" He reached for the tape sealing the box.

"No...it's...I don't know quite what to expect. I mean..."

Chase wrapped his arm around my shoulders. It sent a warm sense of security flowing through my veins. A grin stretched across his lips, which didn't seem apropos. "I can tell you what *not* to expect."

21

I squinted at him, my eyebrows creased. How could he have any idea of what *wasn't* in the box? Mischief glimmered in his eyes. I decided to play along. "Yeah? What's that?"

"A rattlesnake."

I laughed and smacked his chest. "Ya never know."

During the trail drive at Chase's ranch in August, a rattlesnake bit me and a day later I found a rubber snake hidden in my saddle bags.

He winked then dropped his arm from my shoulders. I ripped off the already peeling packing tape then inched open each flap.

A white box big enough to hold a pair of cowboys boots sat at the top. It was labeled *For Sally when she turns 18.*

How could he!

I turned my back to the box, my hands fisted at my side. My anger flared. I closed my eyes and took several deep breaths to help me maintain my composure. I forced myself to remember my father's apology to me and his plea for forgiveness in his dying letter that I'd read a short four days ago. I could not, would not allow this to stir up my anger.

Do not let this get to you, Sally, I told myself. Do not go back to being angry all the time. Being angry at him isn't going to help you in any way, shape, or form. It will only hurt you. Let it go.

"Sally, what's the matter?" Chase asked.

I turned back around and stared down at the words *For Sally when she turns 18.* Why hadn't my father given this to me? Yet another thing for which I needed to forgive him.

I drew in a deep calming breath. "I've never seen this box before. My father never gave it to me."

"Were you still living at home when you turned eighteen?"

"Yeah. I turned eighteen a few months before graduating from high school."

"Should I look through the main box while you examine what's in that one?"

"No, I think probably I'm the best candidate for both." I lifted the white box out of the dish pack and put it in the trunk of my car.

"Aren't you going to look at what's in it?" Chase asked when I returned.

"No, I'll save it for another time when I'm not working against the clock. I've got to finish looking through this other stuff in time for tomorrow's sale." Besides, I was not emotionally prepared to examine that box. The contents promised grief and sadness, and I didn't need any more chaos in my world right now. Instead, I dove into the bigger box of my adoptive mother's things. Dresses, a jewelry box, a well-worn King James Bible. I picked up the Bible and rubbed my hand over its tattered leather binding, then opened it. The inside pages read:

This Holy Bible presented to Helen Ward by her parents on the occasion of her 10th birthday, March 23, 1940.

I turned the page.

Holy Matrimony.

My mother had recorded the details of her marriage. The next few pages contained the *Wife's Family Tree, Husband's Family Tree, Marriages, Births, Deaths.* She'd written names on almost every page.

Lovingly inscribed in perfect penmanship on the page for births was my name, with my birth date and the day I was adopted. Little hearts bookended the adoption date. Tears threatened. A hand on my back startled me. I looked up from the Bible to find Jeremiah next to me.

"She was a good woman, your mom," he said. "The making of your dad."

I scoffed. "I guess that explains why he became so terrible after she died. He reverted back to what he was all along."

"Now don't go talkin' like that," he reprimanded me. "I hear years of bitterness in your voice. For one, you weren't around to know him when he was young. Your dad weren't so bad. But he blamed God for Helen's death and he lost his way after that."

I looked Jeremiah in the eye. I was a relative stranger to him, so it took courage for him to confront me like that. "You're right, of course. Maybe sometime we can sit down and you can tell me about my parents. May I keep this whole box? I'll go through it tonight and bring back anything I don't want in time for tomorrow's sale."

"That's fine." Jeremiah turned to Aaron who sat kicked back on the couch. "Aaron, put this box in Sally's car."

"Sure thing, Grampa." He jumped up.

I placed the Bible back in the box and closed the flaps.

About that time, Abby arrived driving Chase's rental car. "Hey, everybody," she hollered out the window, waving a hand. "I brought lunch."

And just in time. The emotions washing over me threatened to overwhelm me. They ran the gamut from anger at my father to love for my mom who had so obviously cherished the day I arrived in her life.

By now one o' clock had come and gone. I'd been so busy I hadn't even thought about eating. The sun had warmed the air to nearly sixty. Lunch alfresco would be fun.

"Abby, you're an angel." Chase opened the passenger door and grabbed two large brown bags, the Hungry Man's Diner logo adorning the side of each bag. He set them on the kitchen table—my father's furniture came in handy for something. My stomach growled.

"I hope everybody likes beef stew—I know you do, Sally." Abby lifted out two drink containers from one of the bags. "I thought a hot meal would be better than cold sandwiches. There's plenty of coffee and some hot chocolate too."

We took turns dishing stew into paper bowls and pouring our drinks. Contented looks adorned everyone's face. Obviously, we were all hungry and glad for the break.

"Abby, how did your search at the library go?" I took a seat on the couch and set my cup of hot chocolate at my feet.

"Good." She filled her bowl and took a seat beside me. "The accident made front page news, but not for the reason you'd expect. George and Christine Leonard got broadsided by a semi at the highway intersection south of town. The truck driver was drunk, got arrested and was tried for vehicular manslaughter."

"And what about us? Were we in the car?" My throat tightened at her words. I took a sip of hot chocolate to help it relax.

"No, we were at home with a babysitter."

"I remember that accident." Jeremiah's brows knit together as though trying to retrieve the memory. "Made the news for a good week. I knew

George. He owned the feed store. Why would you be searching for—wait a minute. Are you saying you think you're their kids?"

"There's no *think* about it. We found out yesterday," I said firmly. "Ellen Randall over at Hungry Man's Diner told us the day of my father's funeral that we had a brother three years older than us. Ellen was my mom's best friend and looked out for me after Mom died. Mom confided in her that she wanted to adopt all three of us. My father refused. One only, he said. Mom swore Ellen to secrecy about it, but with my father gone, Ellen decided it was time I knew the truth. So we started digging."

Jeremiah shook his head. "I knew he weren't one for kids, but that... well, I'm sorry."

"No need to apologize." Abby scooped a spoonful of stew. "Admittedly, learning we had a brother shocked us. We only discovered each other this past August."

I stood and put my nearly empty bowl of stew on the table. This news of how my biological parents died tainted my appetite.

"Sally..." Chase looked at me. "You didn't tell me that detail about your father allowing only one of you to be adopted. That partly explains your anger when I first saw you last week at his funeral."

"Explains it, but doesn't excuse it." I tried to smile, a bit embarrassed.

"Wow," Aaron said. "I can't imagine what you two must be feeling."

"It's been a tilt-o-whirl ride since July." Abby laid her bowl of stew on her lap and sighed. "My father died and part of his inheritance went to a stranger who turned out to be my twin sister. That's when I learned I was adopted. Sally's adoptive father died last week and we learned we have a brother."

"That's a lot to take in. Can't imagine..." Jeremiah stood, patting his stomach. "That was mighty good food. Thank you. But it's after two. We need to finish the task at hand before it gets dark. How many boxes do you still need to go through, Sally?"

"Only two. It won't take me long." I was grateful for Jeremiah's shift in the conversation. I forced down the rest of my stew and tossed the empty bowl and spoon into the bag it arrived in. Everyone cleared their trash and got back to work.

The western horizon beckoned the sun closer and the temperature descended along with the sun. All the same, Chase and Aaron stripped off their jackets. They were doing the heavy lifting. By 5:30 they had the boxes and furniture neatly stacked back in the large storage unit. Chase and Aaron loaded the cedar chest onto Aaron's pickup, and we headed to the hotel where they carried the chest and the dish box to my room.

We stood in the parking lot to say good-bye. "Jeremiah, thank you for everything. I'll give you a buzz before I leave town. Don't hesitate to call if you need anything. I hope the sale goes well tomorrow."

"It'll be fine. Let's get together for dinner before you leave. I'll tell you about your parents—the Clarks—and what I know about the Leonards."

"I'll call you."

We shook hands, then he and Aaron climbed into the pickup and drove off.

But I wasn't ready to hear about who my father had been before Mom died. How would I reconcile that with the abusive alcoholic I'd known? Jesus had washed away my anger. My experience at the church left no doubt about that. But I functioned out of anger for decades. If I didn't build new patterns of behavior, anger might it rear its ugly head again. I realized a lot of other emotional dominoes had yet to fall.

The three of us trooped to my room. Abby and Chase took a seat at the table, and I plopped down on my bed, worn out physically and emotionally.

"A productive day, I'd say," Chase commented.

"Definitely." Abby let out a contented sigh.

"I'll go through that dish box before bed tonight and store in the cedar chest what I want to keep." I pointed to the box. "The small box will fit in the chest. I'll have it shipped to Great Falls."

"Shipped to Great Falls?" Abby smiled an ear-to-ear toothy grin and delight sparkled in her sky-blue eyes. "Why not shipped home to Kansas City? Is that a Freudian slip? Are you planning to move to Great Falls?"

"Freudian slip? Maybe. Mostly, I figured I'd take a more thorough look at things while I'm there over the holidays." I rose from the bed, grabbed the box from my mom, and put it into the cedar chest.

Abby looked down at it. "For Sally when she turns 18. What's in that?"

"I don't know; I haven't opened it yet."

"You mean—"

"My father never gave it to me. It was in this bigger box marked Helen's Things. My mom's stuff."

"Sally, imagine what might be in there!" Abby eyes widened, and she bent down to pull the box out of the chest.

"No!" I grabbed her arm to stop her, then immediately let go. "I'm sorry if I hurt you. I didn't mean to snap. I expect opening it will come with a lot of hurt and grief. I'm not ready."

"I guess memories of her would stir up grief, but I was thinking about how many answers might be in there."

"Answers to what?" How could a box over forty years old hold answers I needed for today?

"My thoughts exactly." Chase looked up from toying with his Stetson.

"Answers about your adoption. She related the story to Ellen. Maybe she put that and more in a letter to you."

That possibility had never occurred to me. "An interesting thought, but I've been through an emotional tornado—a category EF3 tornado—in the last week. I'm not ready for another one."

Abby turned away from the box and hugged me. "I'm so sorry. I didn't think."

"It's okay. You've been in the storm with me. It can't be easy learning at the age of fifty-eight that you were adopted." I released my hold on Abby, held her at arm's length, and half smiled.

"Why don't I take the chest with me when I fly back to Great Falls?" Chase suggested.

Butterflies invaded my stomach. Were they excited butterflies or fearful? Why would Chase's question prompt them? I didn't want to admit it to anyone—or to myself for that matter—but I was attracted to him. Who wouldn't be with his Harrison Ford handsomeness, brown hair graying at the temples, and muscles that rippled beneath his plaid shirt? "Thanks. That would be a big help. Actually, you can probably head back tomorrow after we meet with Mr. Brown. If he's going to search for our brother's adoption records, I don't see what's left for you to help with."

He glanced at Abby and then back at me. "I told my pilot to enjoy some time off with his wife and new baby. I think I'll stay the weekend at least. Maybe you can show me around your old stomping grounds."

I laughed and plopped back down on the bed. "I've been away for forty years. Not sure I could even find them. Let's clean up and go to dinner. At the moment, I need to put some space between me and that box and clear my head."

Chapter Four

SALLY

"He leads me beside peaceful streams. He
renews my strength." Psalm 23:2b–3a

Friday morning dawned brightly with a ray of sunshine piercing a small opening in the curtains. I actually slept until 7:45. What's with that? I never slept that late, and I had to be at my lawyer's office at nine. Blast, another morning without my run and quiet time with God.

Abby's bed stood empty and made. I assumed she was at breakfast. I dashed to the bathroom for a shower but lingered a few extra seconds under the hot water, allowing it to energize me as I contemplated my day.

Abby still wasn't back when I finished dressing. I grabbed my phone and texted her. She and Chase were at Hungry Man's. I pulled on my hiking boots and coat and walked over to meet them. The heavenly aroma of coffee greeted me when I opened the door to the diner. I paused to enjoy it, then scanned the room to find them.

"Good morning," I chirped. I hooked my purse on the back of the chair and took a seat. "Why didn't you wake me?"

"You, Miss Early Bird, were still asleep at seven. I decided you must need the sleep." Abby poured me a cup of coffee from the pot sitting on the table, a sign we'd become regulars at my friend's restaurant. "Besides, it's not like you have a pressing appointment to get to."

"I meet with Mr. Brown at nine."

Abby pressed her hand across her mouth. "I'm sorry. I forgot about that."

"No harm done. The extra sleep helped, and I still have thirty minutes before I have to be there." I eyed the waffles and sausage links on Chase's plate, then the omelet and toast on Abby's. I leaned over toward Chase and took a deep sniff of the maple syrup his waffles bathed in. He playfully grimaced at me and pulled his plate away. I scowled at him then signaled the waitress with a raise of my eyebrows and tilt of my chin. "I'll have a side of hash browns, please."

She jotted the order on her pad and left.

I doctored my coffee, wrapped my hands around the warm cup, and took a sip, feeling the warmth of it all the way down. "So, Abby, where's Cohen taking you for dinner? We need to get you a new dress." I wiggled my eyebrows.

"Don't be silly." Abby's cheeks flushed pink. "The clothes I have with me are fine. And to answer your question, he didn't say. He's picking me up at six thirty."

"If he didn't say where you're going, how do you know whether to dress casual or fancy?" I asked.

"I'll pick something in between." Abby squinted her eyes, furrowing her eyebrows in the process. But a grin appeared. "What are you up to?"

"Playing matchmaker, what else. I know he's sweet on you." Since Abby was playing matchmaker with me and Chase, then I'd play matchmaker too.

Chase thumped his elbows onto the table, set his chin in his fisted hands, and leaned in. He frowned. "Tell me more about this guy."

"I told you what I know yesterday. He's from here—what are the chances we'd meet someone from Nebraska while stranded in South Dakota?" Abby shook her head as if contemplating the odds. "He's a marketing and brand consultant, though his business is struggling."

The waitress delivered my hash browns and a fresh pot of coffee. I dove in but kept a close eye on Chase and Abby's interaction. Chase looked like a bloodhound on the trail of a bear.

"You didn't tell me that. So he owns his own business?" Chase asked.

"Yes."

"You mentioned he's divorced."

"Yeah. Why does that matter?"

Chase sat back, placing his hands on the table's edge. "Well, I certainly don't want my sister duped by a man who's still married."

His voice held a deep tone of seriousness, but his eyes smiled. Was he teasing or serious? I couldn't tell.

Abby swatted Chase with her napkin, and her cheeks flushed a deeper pink. To me, her embarrassment clearly indicated her attraction to Cohen.

"Enough with the third degree." Abby laughed. "We're having dinner together, not getting engaged."

"Okay, sis, just teasing." Chase cracked a smile, then pointed at Abby. "But I'll remember you said that."

I leaned back in my chair and crossed my arms. I'd never seen this kind of interaction between them before. Is this what having a big brother looking out for you was like? Granted Abby was a grown woman and could take care of herself, but apparently Chase's big-brother instincts were on alert.

"What are you smiling at, Sally?" Chase reached for his coffee.

"Hmm?" I sat forward, my concentration broken. "Didn't realize I was. Just enjoying the banter between you two. Is he always so protective, Abby?"

Abby crossed her arms and took a long look at Chase, her head tilted, eyebrows raised, and lips frowning. Then a smile broke through and she reached over and squeezed Chase's arm. "Yes, he is and I love him all the more for it. He's been a wonderful big brother."

"I wonder what kind of big brother Robert might have been?" The thought saddened me. Had he grown up with a sister or brother. Had life afforded him a second opportunity to be a big brother?

"Thinking about what might have been is a waste of time, Sally. Don't go there." Chase turned his attention to the waffles on his plate.

"You're not *my* big brother, so don't tell me what's a waste of my time," I snarled. Where did that come from?

Chase pulled his head back. "I wondered how long it would be before you groused at me. Is the euphoria from your miracle wearing off already? Your emotional pendulum is enough to give me whiplash."

"Don't you two get started," Abby intervened. "I swear you *like* goading each other. Chase, try and remember Sally grew up an only child, unloved and rejected by her father. She sees the deep love between us. It's only natural she'd wonder what it might have been like had we not been orphaned."

"You're right. ...Sally, I wasn't trying to be bossy. I apologize that it came across that way."

I took a long breath to calm myself. "I'm sorry I snapped. Like I said yesterday, I'm trapped in an emotional tornado. I know thinking about what might have been won't get me anywhere. And don't worry, I'll pay for your chiropractor."

"My chiropractor?"

"To treat your whiplash," I said matter-of-factly and glanced at the clock on the wall. "I'd better get to Mr. Brown's office." I dug $10 out of my purse and dropped it on the table. "This'll cover my hash browns and some of the coffee. Are you still coming with me, Chase?"

I was out the door before he could answer. I checked for traffic then jogged across the street to my car in the hotel parking lot, thankful it didn't take much more than five minutes to get anywhere in town.

Nothing about my life had been normal or routine since I'd received notice of Mr. Reynolds' amazing inheritance to me in July. Chase stirred emotions in me I hadn't felt since my first crush at the age of thirteen. Dealing with men from my foundation of anger had been so much easier than now.

I stood beside the car, closed my eyes, and tilted my face up toward the sunshine while I waited for Chase to catch up. The sun's warmth chased away the chilly air around me. I love you, Lord. I praise and worship You. Thank You for all You do in my life. Calm the storm inside me, heavenly Father, I...I think the anger I operated from also served as an emotional anchor. And now that's gone. I need Your help. *You* are my anchor, my rock, my strong tower I run to in times of trouble. You are my peace.

"Good morning, Miss Clark," the receptionist greeted me when Chase and I entered Mr. Brown's office. "Mr. Brown is with someone at the moment but should be free in the next minute or two. Have a seat." She motioned toward a tan love seat and matching accent chair lining one wall.

I took the chair and scanned the office. Chase stood at the window, probably watching the happenings along the street. Or was he lost in thought and staring at nothing? It didn't matter. What did was that he wasn't sitting right beside me.

I had failed to observe Mr. Brown's office when I was here last week so I took the opportunity to look around. One wall was red brick, giving the room a modern feel yet reminiscent of another era as well. Light beige paint covered the other three walls with a large picture of the Scotts Bluff National Monument on the north wall. The large life-like painting gave me the sense of looking out a picture window. A Xerox printer occupied the wall opposite me. It busily churned out collated pages—from another era for sure. Several cases of paper were stacked next to it. What an interesting juxtaposition of the past and present. The receptionist's area engulfed a third of the room. Clean, tidy, and cozy. I rather liked it.

"Sally?"

The voice plucked me from my observations, and I looked in its direction. "Cohen? What are you doing here?" I stood and walked over to greet him, Chase trailing me.

"Mark is my brother-in-law. What are *you* doing here?" Cohen answered, astonished. He wore a well-cut coal black suit with a white shirt and cobalt blue tie. I had to give the man credit; he was an impeccable dresser. His fit and trim stature didn't hurt either. I fully understood Abby's attraction. Were it not for his abrasive personality, I might have been attracted to him too. Standing next to Cohen, Mr. Brown appeared rather frumpy in what was probably an off-the-rack brown suit with matching tie and cream shirt. Not that Mr. Brown was frumpy, but anyone would look that way next to Cohen in his tailor-made thousand dollar suit.

"Mr. Brown is handling my father's estate."

"Good morning, Miss Clark." Mr. Brown shook my hand. He turned to Cohen. "Is Miss Clark the crazy woman who was snowed in with you and Hannah?"

That got a laugh from Chase. Had Mr. Brown meant to say *crazy* or was it a slip of the tongue? "Yup, I'm that crazy woman."

"I only said that *at first* I thought you were crazy." Cohen's cheeks turned bright red. "I'm still amazed at what happened." He shook his head. "Who's this with you?"

"This is Chase Reynolds, Abby's brother by adoption. Chase, this is Cohen Reed and Mark Brown."

"Nice to meet you." Chase shook hands with each and politely smiled.

"My, what a small world." Mr. Brown looked at Cohen, then turned to me. "What can I do for you, Miss Clark? It's too soon for your father's death certificates to have arrived."

"Oh, I realize that. I came on another matter." Small world? Tiny seemed more appropriate. "Cohen, Abby's at Hungry Man's Diner having breakfast. Why don't you join her?" I encouraged him.

Cohen glanced at Mr. Brown, then at his watch, then at Chase. "I suppose I have a bit of time even though I'll see her tonight. Mr. Reynolds, it was nice to meet you. Sally, in a town this size, I expect I'll see you around."

Cohen left and Mr. Brown ushered Chase and me into his private office. "What matter can I help you with, Miss Clark?" He took a seat at his mahogany desk. I admired the intricate carvings along each panel and the feet. A matching coat tree stood in the corner behind him and held a gray knee length wool overcoat and ragged gray bucket hat.

"Abby and I learned last week that we have a brother. I'd like you track down his adoption records."

He pulled a Pilot Falcon gold nib fountain pen from the inside breast pocket of his suit. I recognized the pen because I researched them back in the day when I still imagined myself a bestselling author signing my books in style. I shook the image from my head.

"He'd be about sixty-one now, three years older than Abby and I. We were adopted from Lowenfeld Home for Orphans. His name is Robert. Our biological parents were George and Christine Leonard."

"I remember Lowenfeld's." He slipped on a pair of plastic black-frame glasses, the kind that in the Marine Corps earned the nickname birth-control glasses because they were so ugly. Somehow they suited him. He opened his fountain pen, pulled a legal pad to the center of his desk, and jotted some notes. "The orphanage shut down many years ago, but this information is a good start. Is there a medical necessity or you simply want to find your brother?"

"Just want to find him." I shrugged. "Why do you ask about medical necessity?"

"Nebraska has sealed adoption records. Medical necessity is the most common reason adoption records are opened." He leaned back in his black leather chair, pulled off his glasses, and chewed on one tip. "Do you know anything about your birth parents besides their names?"

"Only that they were killed in a car accident, which is what orphaned us."

"That makes a difference as well." He slipped on his glasses again and made several more notes on his legal pad.

"How much time do you think this'll take?" Chase asked before I could.

"That's difficult to say. I'll have to start with the county court, most likely file a petition. I expect a good month or more."

I frowned then shrugged. "It is what it is. Until last week we didn't even know we had a brother. How much help does knowing our parents make?" Why did the desire to find my brother burn with greater intensity each day that passed?

"I honestly don't know. The last adoption I dealt with was twenty years ago, and it was to help a couple adopt a child. I'll do my best."

"Do you need a retainer?"

"No."

"But you're already handling my father's stuff. I need to pay you for that as well."

"That's been covered by a security retainer your father paid many years ago. My hourly rate is $250. I'll have my clerk send you a bill when needed. How long do you anticipate being in town?"

"I have no idea. At least until I get the death certificates."

"Excellent. I'll have my clerk call you when they arrive. I expect they'll be here by early next week."

I stood and reached across the desk to shake his hand. "Thank you so much for your time, Mr. Brown. And what a surprise that Cohen is your brother-in-law. A small world indeed."

He rose from his chair and clasped my hand. "Call me Mark." He showed us out of his office and to the front door.

I had planned to rejoin Abby at the diner, but I didn't want to interrupt any time she and Cohen might have together. I'd never had a boyfriend, but I'd seen *Fiddler on the Roof* enough times to know for romance to develop they needed time together.

"Let's head back to the diner. I want to check out this Cohen guy," Chase said as we made our way to the car.

"Let them enjoy time together alone. You act like the man is a wolf in sheep's clothing or something." I unlocked the car and climbed in.

"I saw the deep red blush on his face when he asked about her. That's enough indication for me."

Chapter Five
CHASE

"Cry out for insight, and ask for understanding." Proverbs 2:3

Abby wasn't at the diner when Sally and I got there so we returned to her hotel room.

"Abby?" Sally called the moment she opened the door. "I'm here!"

"You'll never guess who we saw at Mr. Brown's office." Sally bounded into the room like a dog too-long penned in her kennel.

Abby lounged in bed, knees up, a book in her lap. She looked up at Sally, her lips pressed together as though suppressing a smile. "Cohen."

Sally's shoulders drooped. "Ahh, I was hoping to surprise you."

"So he did stop by the diner. Did he stay long?" I tossed my Stetson on the table and took a seat.

"Yes, he stopped but didn't stay long. Why?"

"I was hoping to get better acquainted with him." I squinted at Abby and pointed my finger at her. "Sally's right; he's smitten with you."

"What's with you two and the word *smitten*?" Sally tossed her coat on the bed, unlaced her boots, then sat on the bed and tugged them off. "Is that some Montana thing?"

Boots off, Sally squirmed around on the bed, reminding me of a dog circling before lying down. She finally propped a pillow up on the headboard and settled in. I shook my head to chase away the golden retriever image.

Abby snickered, placed a bookmark into her book, and closed it. "No, it isn't. And no, Cohen is not smitten with me."

"If I remember correctly that's the same thing I said to you, Abby, when you said Chase was smitten with me."

My mouth dropped open. I raised an eyebrow at Abby. "And just when did you tell her this?"

"After I went to Kansas City to Sally's place to help her with her business deal."

"She did," Sally reiterated. "But don't forget, Chase, you told me in August you thought you were falling in love with me. So I'm not sure why I insisted you weren't smitten."

"Yes, I remember. I, uh…didn't realize anyone had noticed. Dear Abby," I shook my head at her, "always the observant one. Did Cohen tell you he's Mark Brown's brother-in-law?"

Abby bolted up from her half-prone position on the bed. "No, he didn't. The coincidences keep piling up."

"What coincidences?" I asked.

"The *coincidence* of checking into a hotel across the street from a diner that Sally's childhood friend now owns," Abby ticked them off on her fingers, "meeting said friend at the diner who tells us we have a brother, meeting someone from Sally's hometown of Scottsbluff while stranded in South Dakota, and now discovering that person is brother-in-law to Sally's lawyer."

"When you put it that way…" I said, my eyes wide.

"What's the next surprise God has up His sleeve?" Sally jumped off the bed. "I never got through that box last night. If I plan to take any of it to Jeremiah, I need to get at it." She tipped her head toward the large box of her mother's things.

"Do you want some help?" Abby swung her feet to the floor.

"No. It shouldn't take me long."

I rose from my seat at the table. "I'd like to call home and make sure all's well at the ranch. We have several pregnant mares; I want to make sure they're doing well."

"And I'll check in and see how things are running at the magazine."

Abby grabbed her phone from the bedside table.

"Then we've all got something to do. Great." Sally turned her attention to the box.

The cold weather streak had disappeared, melting the majority of the snow, so Abby and I went out to the patio. I caught her up on things at the ranch, then we each made our respective phone calls, she with my daughter Emily at *Cattle & Cowboy* magazine and me with my son Michael. The mares were doing fine.

Watching and interacting with Sally the past two days had been like meeting her for the first time. She'd lost her hardness and some of her guarded stance. Even Abby seemed different. I'm sure they realized they'd come out of their blizzard miracle as new women, but was the transformation as stark to them as it was to me?

"All done." Sally poked her head out the sliding door.

"That didn't take long." Abby put down the book she'd been reading since finishing her call with Emily. "Wasn't painful, was it?"

"No. I didn't recognize much of what was in the box. I put what little I wanted to keep in the cedar chest and took the rest to Jeremiah. Lots of people already there for the auction." Sally stepped out onto the patio and slid the door shut behind her.

"Good, maybe he won't have to cart anything to Goodwill." I pocketed my phone.

"I hadn't even noticed you leave," Abby said.

Sally hesitatingly stepped toward the table. "I, uh…I think you two should consider heading back home to Great Falls tomorrow."

"Why are you so anxious to get rid of us?" I held my hands out palms up to punctuate my *why*.

"Obviously you're needed at home, and there's nothing left for you to help with. I'm just waiting on death certificates, and the lawyer is handling the search for Robert. Abby, you've been away from work for a month now. Surely, you're antsy to get back."

"Not really."

Sally tilted her head and raised one eyebrow. "Seriously?"

"Yes, seriously. Is that your only objection?"

"I'm way out of my comfort zone here." Sally's cheeks flushed red.

I laughed. "My presence makes you nervous, doesn't it?"

Sally nodded.

"How are you going to manage for the next two months at the ranch with me constantly around?" I asked.

"Spend my time in the barn with the horses, hiding." Sally smirked.

"Do all men make you nervous or just me?"

Sally's forehead wrinkled. She crossed her arms, a sure sign she intended to keep the answer locked behind those soft pink lips of hers.

Abby rose and headed into the room. Sally and I followed.

"Where are my black pants?" Abby rooted around in her suitcase.

"What do you need your black pants for?" Sally joined Abby. No doubt, Sally was glad to change the subject.

"For my date tonight. Did my pants get mixed in with your clothes?" They went to Sally's suitcase and perused the contents. Abby shook her head. "Maybe I left them at your place, Sally. I guess I'll have to wear my pink suit."

"Why? We've got time, so let's go shopping and get something that'll knock Cohen's socks off." Sally rubbed her hands together and smiled mischievously. What did she have up her sleeve? I didn't necessarily want to discourage the relationship between Abby and Cohen but didn't feel inclined to encourage it either. Did long distance relationships ever work out?

"I do not want to *knock off* any clothing, thank you very much. It needs to stay exactly where it belongs."

"Oh come on, you know what I mean. Don't you want to wow him?" Sally insisted.

Abby's cheeks turned pink. Was she truly attracted to this man? She'd kept men at arm's length since getting left at the altar thirty years ago. I needed to get better acquainted with this guy, and soon.

"Shopping for a new outfit sounds like a good idea." I stepped forward. "Your pink suit is fine for work, Abby, but not for a date. Aaaand, it'll give Sally a break from me, since I make her nervous."

"You make Sally nervous? What are you talking about?"

Apparently, Abby's thoughts had been elsewhere—on Cohen?—during part of our earlier conversation. I smiled at her. "Never mind. Go shopping."

I had four hours to contrive an excuse to be around when Cohen arrived.

Chapter Six

SALLY

"I trust in you, my God! Do not let me be disgraced." Psalm 25:2

A dress hadn't graced my body in decades—give me a pair of blue jeans any day—so who was I to say what Abby needed for her date. After some quick searching on the Internet, we found a boutique and headed off.

"Good afternoon. How can I help you?" the eager clerk asked when we entered. I stared at her a moment. Only car salesmen ever greeted me. But then again, I did most of my shopping at Walmart.

"I'd like to look around for a bit, first," Abby said. "But thank you."

"Very well. I'll be right here if you need any assistance." The clerk smiled politely and resumed her position behind the counter.

"I don't see why the clothes I brought for church aren't good enough for my date," Abby whispered as we made our way farther into the store.

"Humor me." I meandered to a rack of dresses. Lots of glitter, certainly not my style. But Abby's? "Do you like glittery or the classic look?"

"Classic, definitely. I'm pragmatic too. I'd like something that will double for a special work function, not just a date."

"Mmmm?" I rocked my head from side to side. "I'm okay with that."

We perused the store for several minutes. Strapless, frilly cocktail dresses that would barely cover the necessities occupied one corner. In another, shimmery long-sleeve floor-length dresses. I always wondered who designed women's clothing. Men who wanted to ogle what they could or women who felt exposing themselves an essential part of attracting of man? I hated shopping for clothes.

While I walked the floor, I got a text from Chase. *I want a few words with Cohen before he takes Abby out. Expect me at your room at 6:25. I'll take you to dinner afterwards.*

"Anything wrong?" Abby asked.

I looked up from my phone. "No, just Chase texting he'd take me to dinner. Mind, not asking, but telling me."

Abby snickered. "In that case, this would be perfect for you." She held up a sapphire blue form-fitting, long-sleeve, mid-calf dress with no scoop to the neckline. The color alone grabbed my attention.

"That's gorgeous, but we're here to shop for you, not me." I frowned and pointed for her to put the dress back on the rack as if admonishing a four-year-old.

"You're no fun." She huffed but complied.

"Wait a minute. Why not that dress for you?" I walked over, pulled the dress from the rack, and put it up against her. "It's gorgeous."

"I'd prefer it in pink." She took the dress from me and put it back on the rack yet again, then planted her hands on her hips. "You know, in the whole three months since we met, I've never seen you wear a dress. Do you even own one?"

I shut my eyes, tilted my head up and to the left, and pictured the clothes in my closet. I knew what hung there, nothing but pants, shirts, and suit coats. I could always claim my Marine Corps dress blue uniform. I doubted Abby would accept that argument. I opened my eyes and smirked at her. "Nope. I don't like dresses."

"Why not?"

I shrugged. "Don't know. Just never have."

"I'll make you a deal then." Abby had that mischievous look on her face again, one I was growing familiar with.

I crossed my arms and cocked my eyebrow at her. "I'm listening."

"I'll buy a dress to wow Cohen, if you'll buy a dress to wow Chase."

I never should have told her Chase was taking me to dinner. How was I going to get out of this?

I stared at myself in the hotel bathroom mirror. I'd question this purchase for the rest of my life. What an insult to this beautiful sophisticated blue dress to drape it over my straight-as-a-board figure. Like putting a formal gown on a scarecrow. I didn't have any of the right curves. Besides, what kind of message would Chase think I was sending? This wasn't an official date, was it? "Abby, this was a terrible idea."

Abby entered the bathroom. "You look gorgeous. Slinky, even. Wish I had your figure."

"Like a stick, you mean? Running three miles a day helps."

"Not gonna happen. And you don't look like a stick! Let's add some mascara, blush, and a bit of curl to your hair." She plugged in her curling iron, then rooted around in her toiletry bag for the mascara and blush. "Here," she handed me the items, "you do know how to put these on, right?"

"If I search my brain's archive, I might figure it out." And it would require searching the archive.

Abby laughed, then proceeded to curl my hair. How she would manage to curl my two-inch-long hair was a mystery to me.

"This dress demands curves I've never had and never will. Tell me again, why did I let you talk me into this?" I wrapped my arms around my waist. A sensation of vulnerability permeated my gut and burned like a hot poker.

"Because you want me to impress Cohen." She released the first curl and started on another.

"Oh yeah. But this isn't me, Abby. I feel like...like..." The truth hurt too much to admit.

"Like what?" Abby released the second curl and deftly started another.

"How can I say this? I know your heart's in the right place, but..." I swallowed the words I wanted to say. I felt like a fake. I wasn't pretty and no amount of dress-up would change that. "I don't want to give Chase the wrong impression."

"Isn't the idea to let Chase know you're interested?"

"No. This was your idea."

"But aren't you interested?"

"Kind of, but this…it's too much."

Finished with curling my hair, Abby set the iron on the counter, fluffed the curls with her fingers, then stood back to examine her handiwork in the mirror. "You're beautiful, Sally. Don't you at least feel pretty?"

"I do. But all pretty ever accomplished was to create a line of Marines who wanted sex. I feel like a hooker," I blurted. I hadn't meant to say any of that, despite its truth.

"Oh, Sally. I'm so sorry. You most certainly are not that. And you haven't painted the Marines in a good light either."

"I know all men aren't that way, but that was my experience during many of my years in the Corps."

Abby gripped my shoulders and turned me to face her. "You are a beautiful woman, inside and out. It's time to root out all lies that say otherwise. You are created in God's image. Do you imagine Him to be like those Marines?"

"I…I never thought about it that way before."

"Our life experiences so often taint our view of God. You are His child and He loves you dearly. You know that in your head," she tapped my temple with her finger, "but you need to keep telling yourself until it sinks deep into your heart." She briefly held her hand over my heart, then shifted it back to my shoulder.

I nodded. "You're right. Old habits die hard, as they say."

"It's not about habits. It's about what you believe deep in your subconscious. We both know men are affected by physical appearances. But Chase puts more store in the condition of your heart, just like God does." Abby shifted her hands from my shoulders to my face. "And it's the condition of your heart the people around you pick up on. *You* can create the life you want for yourself, but you have to stop quenching the authentic you God created you to be."

I closed my eyes and took a deep breath. I wanted to experience the abundant life Jesus promised, but create my own life? Find the real me? I looked at Abby. "It's going to take a lot of digging to do that."

She squeezed my face then dropped her hands. "That's okay. Just be sure to do it so you can step into all God has promised you." She pulled her new dress from the hanger on the back of the bathroom door. "It's a good thing Chase won't be up on a horse when he sees you, otherwise, he'd fall off."

"You really think so?" I kinda liked that idea, and the humor I found in picturing it relieved the tension I'd created in the air.

"Yes, I do."

I sighed. "Enough. You'd think we were eighteen years old again."

"Who says fun is restricted to teenagers? Now help me with my dress. They'll both be here soon."

At exactly 6:25 I heard a knock at the door. I figured it was Chase, but I didn't want to answer it. I froze at my place by the table, as though standing at attention in front of the commanding general. I wasn't ready to face him.

"That's probably Chase." Abby slipped her heels on. "Let me answer. I want to see his face when he sees you." She went to the door. I had a straight line of vision and nervously watched to see who it would be.

"Hi, Abby. You look gorgeous!" Cohen's eyebrows nearly reached his hairline and his eyes bugged out. "Perfect for where I planned to take you. Shall we go?"

Abby reached for the winter coat she'd bought along with the dress.

"Wait a minute," I hollered and stepped halfway to the door. How could I stall them long enough for Chase to get here?

"Sally, is that you?" Cohen's eyebrows made an abrupt drop to the bridge of his nose.

"Of course, it's me!" That man exasperated me.

"You look so…different."

"You have Abby to thank for that. This is *not* the real me."

"Hello again, Cohen."

Cohen's surprise over my looks afforded the time needed for Chase to appear. I recognized his voice but couldn't see him from my position in the room.

Cohen turned away from Abby. "Chase, wasn't it? Abby's brother?"

"Yes," Abby said. "He's here helping us take care of Sally's father's estate."

"Nice to meet you again, Chase. Maybe we can get better acquainted while you're here in town."

Cohen's geniality with Chase surprised me. Cohen had been so panicked the whole time we were stranded that his friendly, calm demeanor now didn't jive with what I knew of him.

"I'd like that. Maybe some time this weekend. I'm only in town for a few days," Chase said. "At the moment, I'm here to take Sally to dinner."

Abby stepped into the hallway and Chase stepped into her place in the doorway. I held my breath waiting for his reaction. Our eyes met briefly, then he leaned into the hallway presumably to watch Abby and Cohen depart.

How disappointing was that! I knew this had been a terrible idea. I nearly bolted for the bathroom to wash off the makeup and change clothes except I would have to pass Chase to get there. Steady, Marine, stand your ground. Waiting for a grenade to explode was less nerve-racking.

Finally, Chase stepped into the room, shut the door, and looked at me.

"Holy cow!" He stepped up to me, grabbed my hand, and slowly twirled me around.

My heart knocked my vocal chords out of place as he admired me.

I felt his eyes on me much the same way I'd felt them at our first meeting over dinner in Kansas City. I suspected then he wasn't impressed with what he saw. What was he thinking now?

His turquoise and black western shirt, black pants, and Stetson dumped a passel of butterflies loose in my stomach.

"I thought the idea was to wow Cohen, not me."

"That's what I told Abby, but she insisted I buy a dress, too, or she wouldn't. What choice did I have?"

"None, I guess, if you insist on playing matchmaker. I had to bite my tongue to keep from reacting when I first saw you. Didn't want to give Abby any fodder for teasing me with later."

"Who's to say I won't tell her?"

"No one. …Sally. " He took another step closer to me, so close his minty warm breath caressed my cheek. His eyes locked on mine. "I… You're dressed much too fancy for Hungry Man's, and I'm in the mood for a steak. Where should we go?" He turned abruptly and headed to the door.

What had he intended to say and couldn't? Or had he wanted to kiss me?

Chapter Seven

CHASE

"Wise choices will watch over you. Understanding
will keep you safe." Proverbs 2:11

The clatter of plates and silverware, the roar of a hundred voices, and loud country-western music assaulted my ears the moment I opened the door of the steakhouse for Sally. No promise of a quiet evening, but then I hadn't given the evening much thought beyond how awkward I felt. The last woman I took out to dinner was my wife. Five years had passed since her death.

Waiting customers jammed the lobby. We maneuvered our way through the crowd to the waiter's station. "Table for two, please."

The waiter consulted the seating chart. "It'll be about a twenty minute wait, sir."

"You okay with that, Sally?"

"Guess we'll have to be. It's Friday, probably every restaurant in town has a wait list."

I turned back to the waiter, my eyebrows raised.

"Name?"

"Reynolds."

He jotted it down and handed me a pager.

"Let's go outside to wait. It'll be less crowded," Sally hollered as she leaned toward my ear, then promptly headed to the door, weaving between the milling people in the lobby.

"Let's hope the crowd is an indication of how good the food is. At least it isn't cold out tonight." I motioned Sally to an empty bench by the door and we took a seat to wait.

I gazed at her, from the curls I'd never seen in her light brown hair to the dazzling blue dress to the black pumps she wore. I marveled at the transformation of the plain Jane I'd met in early August. I remembered thinking *she's no show heifer.* How could I have been so crass? Abby was a beautiful woman and Sally was her identical twin, yet that beauty didn't shine through when I first met her. Pop certainly knew what he was doing adding the stipulation that Sally spend four weeks at the ranch in order to claim the inheritance he'd given her. After five days on the trail drive that first week at the ranch, a transformation had begun. Now after her encounter with Jesus, a beautiful new woman had emerged and I found myself mesmerized by her.

"Chase!"

I blinked several times to bring my thoughts back to the present moment. "What?"

"I know my *dazzling appearance* has left you speechless, but would you please answer my question?" She sat with her mouth open, her palms up.

Question? What question? "Why do you that?"

"Do what?"

"Be snarky at me so often? You *are* dazzling, so don't cut yourself down like that. You're insulting God when you do. He created you. Do you think He sees you as anything but beautiful?" That she'd butted heads with Cohen didn't surprise me. It was all we'd done practically from the first day I met her. Getting close to Sally was like hugging a porcupine. Why was she so prickly all the time?

Despite that, my attraction to her had grown, but I didn't desire a sparring partner. I hadn't given the evening much thought, but I had hoped for a pleasant meal with pleasant conversation, not a boxing match.

She shut her eyes and took a deep breath. What was she thinking? Was she struggling to believe that God sees her as beautiful? Was she trying to calm down to keep herself from grousing at me.?

"Never mind."

Not the response I expected. I sensed an air of resignation, something I'd never experienced from her. Her fighting spirit had, as she would say it, gone AWOL. Had the emotional turmoil of the past three months taken its toll? "I'm sorry, I was lost in thought. Can you repeat your question?"

"How hard would it be to gain access to police records?"

"I have no idea. What records do you want and why?" I toyed with the pager to keep myself from staring at Sally.

"I want to find out more about the accident the Leonards were in."

"Why? What would the accident tell you about them?"

"I...I don't know. But want to know who I am and where I came from. I just figured that would be a place to start."

Life had denied her of her biological parents. Of course she wanted to find out more about them. "It might be, but I don't imagine the police are in the habit of turning records over to complete strangers with no connection to the case."

"No connection? I'm their daughter!"

Patience, man. She's walking an emotional tightrope right now. "Yes, that's true."

Her hands sat folded in her lap. I draped an arm behind her and over the top of the bench. I put my other hand over her hands, hoping its warmth would bring her some calm. She looked at me then pulled an index finger free and laid it on top of my hand. Again, not a response I expected, but I took it as a good sign that she acknowledged my intent.

"I know this is hard, Sally, but without whatever paperwork Karl uncovered, you have nothing to prove that. The police rarely even tell the press all the details. You were in the military police in the Marines. I'd have thought you'd know the process."

"The government is an entity unto its own. With its own rules. Don't you know that?" Sally scoffed and pulled her hands from mine. "The only information *they* willingly give is where to find the head."

"Where to find your head? What?"

"*The* head. That's Marine-speak for bathroom."

I laughed. "I'm sure they're willing to give more information than that."

Sally frowned at me, tilted her head down and to one side, and cocked one eyebrow—a look I was beginning to recognize as her "you've got to be kidding me" response. "How did you become so cynical?"

"*You* spend fifteen years in the military—as a woman—and see if you don't get a tad cynical. When I joined up, feminism was still in its infancy. A lot of men didn't want to serve with women. As far as they were concerned, women were there to serve *their* needs, if you get my drift."

Was that what she thought of all men? Had any in particular taken advantage of her? Was that why I made her nervous?

The pager buzzed, startling me. I lifted the pager so she could see its blinking red light. "Table's ready."

We made our way into the restaurant, the waiter ushered us to a table, and handed us each a menu. We took our seats, Sally burying herself in the menu. It offered me time to regroup. I knew so little of her and struggled to get my head around what I did know. Would it be a safe bet to assume she didn't trust any man? This tidbit of information certainly helped me make sense of her combative behavior in August and initial skepticism about Pop's inheritance.

"Good evening, folks. What can I get you to drink?" the waitress asked.

"Just water for me. Thank you," Sally said.

"Same here."

She nodded and left. I turned my attention to the menu, during which time my ears adjusted to the restaurant's noise level. "I think I'll have the T-bone. How 'bout you?"

"The filet mignon looks good." She set her menu to the side.

The waitress brought our drinks, took our order, and hurried off.

"So, back to our conversation," Sally said. "It's been fifty-eight years since the accident that killed the Leonards. What would it matter to the police who I am and why I want the information?"

"Sally, I honestly don't know." I shrugged and leaned back in my chair. "Why don't you call the police station in the morning and ask, or if you like, we can go down there together."

She took a long drink of water. A stalling tactic? What answer did she expect from me? She set down her glass and made eye contact. "Why does the legal system make things so hard? I know nothing about the family I came from. I have a brother out there somewhere and neither of us are getting any younger. My adoptive father's rejection left me feeling alone in the world, and I'm tired of being alone."

I had to bite my tongue to stop my initial response, one that would have probably been hurtful and delivered in haste.

Truth could hurt sometimes, but I would temper it the way Pop had taught me to approach difficult truths. I took a moment to collect my thoughts.

"Sally, my relationship with you is important to me. You're Abby's twin sister and part of the family now. I want to get to know you better, and being truthful is essential to any relationship. Would you agree?"

She squinted one eye and cocked the other eyebrow. "Yes. …Am I about to be drawn and quartered?"

"No, of course not. But I have something difficult to share. May I?"

She stared at me for several moments. "I'm a Marine. I think I can take it."

"A Marine caught in an emotional tornado as you described it. I don't want to possibly add to it without your permission."

"So I go from a Cat. EF3 to an EF4. I'll manage." She unrolled the silverware nestled in a cloth napkin and laid the steak knife and fork on the table and the napkin in her lap.

The waitress appeared with our steaks. Impeccable timing that allowed my nerves to calm a bit. I had a tough truth to share and expected a nasty response from Sally. I waited until the waitress left before I proceeded.

"You're alone because you won't let anyone in. And you blame your dad for all your problems." Despite the warmth in which I'd spoken, my words seemed to hang in the air like a vulture circling a dying animal.

I watched Sally's face for emotional indications of how strong her reaction might be. I expected her ubiquitous snarky comment, but none came. Maybe being in a restaurant kept her mouth shut. Maybe it took all her strength to keep herself under control.

"Can you share what you heard me say?"

"That I won't let people in and I blame my father for everything." What did her blank stare mean?

"Yes. How do you feel about that?"

"What? Am I on the psychiatrist's couch now?" She sliced into her filet, screeching the plate as she did. She cringed, put down her silverware, and briefly closed her eyes.

"No I'm not psychoanalyzing you. You have a right to express your feelings about what I said. How you feel is important to *you*, and it's important to *me*."

She sighed. "I've never had things presented to me like that before. It's thrown me off balance. I know I don't let people in very easily, but where my father is concerned, I'll have to think about that one. Thank you for telling me."

Her calm response shocked me, throwing me a bit off balance with her. "When you blame others for your troubles, you make yourself a victim. Is God ever a victim?"

"Of course not."

"So think about it. God is a creator, and you're created in His image. He created you to be like Him. Would He want you to always behave like a victim?" Would she understand I was trying to help her grow rather than tearing her down?

She sat staring at me. "Probably not."

"God gave us the choice of life or death. To choose life is to be a creator, to create the life He set before us. Being a victim is choosing death." I paused and let her ponder that.

"Why are you telling me this? What are you after?"

"I'm not after anything. I simply want to see you grow in who you are in Christ. He died to bring you abundant life. Is that what you've been living?"

She stared at the food on her plate while she absentmindedly rubbed at the condensation on her dinner glass. A habit of hers I had learned from the first day we met during dinner in Kansas City.

I'd given her a lot to think about. Would she accept what I'd said and truly think about it? Time to change tack. "Didn't Jeremiah say he knew George Leonard and that he owned a feed store? Why not talk to him?"

Sally nodded and scooped up some rice pilaf. "Good idea."

I took her calm demeanor as a good sign. Either that or she was pulling on every bit of self-control she had within her. "In the meantime, can you tell me about Cohen?"

"If you're trying to change the subject, smart move." She gave me a half-smile and sliced another bite of steak.

I sighed. A smile, small though it was, another good sign.

"I have little good to say about Cohen."

"What? Abby's on a date with this guy—that you encouraged—and you have nothing good to say. Is he going to break her heart?" I sliced into my T-bone and took a bite.

Sally leaned across the table. "Chase, I honestly don't know."

I didn't know whether to laugh or scowl at her for throwing my own words back at me. But I glimpsed a glint of her fighting spirit returning. "Elucidate. What's wrong with the guy?"

"Nothing I suppose, but we butted heads the whole time we were stranded. Every time I turned around he was calling me crazy for seeing the church differently than he did." She sat tall. "Abby saw it the same way I did, but he never called *her* crazy. His mood was as up and down as an elevator. Honestly, a lot of his behavior reminded me of my father."

That explained a lot.

"He did eventually apologize. Maybe it's just my general distrust of men." She speared some broccoli, but with the fork midway to her mouth she stopped and pointed it at me, broccoli and all. "And I don't want to see Abby get hurt anymore than you do."

"I'm glad we can agree on something."

We finished eating, mostly in silence, and I paid the bill.

"Thank you for dinner," Sally said as we strode to the door. "I'm sorry I wasn't more enjoyable company."

"I enjoyed your company just fine, and you're welcome." We exited the steakhouse into the crisp fall air of the evening. I took a deep breath. "It's a beautiful evening, and the night is young. Why don't we go for a walk or a take in a movie?"

"A walk would be nice, but let's make it short. I feel worn out tonight."

Emotional turmoil could do that to you. All the same, her agreement surprised me, but then again she constantly surprised me. I half expected snarky comments from her, but her calm acceptance of what I'd said tonight showed me God was at work in her. Knowing her made every day an adventure. Would that ever change? She took life by the horns and faced who-knows-what while in the military, yet my presence unnerved her. What a conundrum.

"Is a turn around the block short enough?"

"That works."

I didn't know whether to take her arm in mine or not, so I just started a slow walk and she fell in beside me. We strolled down the sidewalk in silence. I smiled and nodded at the people we passed, many of whom were laughing and enjoying the evening. Eventually, Sally hooked her arm in mine, but never said a word until we rounded the last corner.

"Chase, I'm more than ready to change into my pajamas, climb into bed, and watch an oldies movie on TV. Do you mind?"

"Of course not," I lied. We walked to the car and drove back to the hotel.

"How about tomorrow we visit the Scotts Bluff National Monument? Maybe Abby will come with us, if she and Cohen aren't on another date."

"Sounds like a plan." We entered the hotel and I escorted Sally to her room. "So, you don't want to go down to the police station first to find out about the Leonards?"

"No, I'll give them a call sometime in the next several days."

She unlocked her door and pushed it part way open but stood looking at me. Apprehension clouded her eyes. Did she expect a goodnight kiss? Surely not. But I wanted to give one. I wanted to know what those soft pink lips would taste like.

"Good night," she finally said. "Thanks again for dinner."

"You're welcome. Sleep well." I walked down the hall to my room, disappointed at not spending more of the evening with her, even if it meant snarky comments and emotional turmoil.

Chapter Eight
SALLY

"Feel my pain and see my trouble. Forgive all my sins." Psalm 25:18

Chase waited as I unlocked the door and said good night. His energy level telegraphed his desire for a kiss. I read it in his eyes as well. What message had my eyes held? That was anybody's guess because at this point I was clueless about what I wanted. I watched him walk down the hallway to his room, noting his disappointment in the droop of his shoulders.

Duh, Sally, he suggested a movie or a walk because he wanted to spend more time with you. Of course he's disappointed.

I pulled my eyes from Chase and pushed the door the rest of the way open, only to be greeted by darkness. No doubt, Abby was still out with Cohen. Was she enjoying herself?

I doubt her date played out as awkward as mine. Forget being eighteen again. This could rival the awkwardness of a young girl's first date. But then had Chase considered it a date? Our conversation didn't reflect that. I laid my purse and car keys on the desk and doffed my coat and shoes.

Like Chase said, the night was young, only eight o' clock, yet my brain screamed sleep deprivation. I enjoyed our walk and wanted it to be longer, but my body felt like a platoon of Marines had collided with me during their morning ten-mile run to the base gate and back. Not only that, my emotions felt as wrung out as a dishrag.

61

I slipped off my dress and hung it up. Would I ever be able to wear that dress again? I'd forever connect it to this date with Chase. The night hadn't been a catastrophe but neither had it been fireworks. Had I expected fireworks? As I thought about it, I drew a blank.

I clicked on the TV and slipped into my PJs while I replayed Chase's words about victim and creator, that choosing life was to create the life you wanted. Most certainly I had not expected a conversation like that.

Twice in the span of two hours I'd been told I could create the life I wanted. Was that true?

I wearily crawled into bed. Scrolling through the channels, I discovered only Halloween movies populated the television. That made sense. October 31 was only ten days away. But I'd experienced enough real horror in my life, and there was nothing entertaining about it.

You blame your dad for all your problems.

I had used all the self-discipline I could muster to stop myself from snapping at Chase over that one. No way did I want to create an angry scene in the restaurant. Why did I lose tongue control when I was around him? Not only did I lose control of my tongue, but also of my emotions. Why? Maybe his initial rudeness when we first met played a role. He and his lawyer, Karl Kandell, had flown to Kansas City to review the inheritance Chase's father had given me. He'd looked at me like I was a cow to be culled from his herd. Still, his observation rated consideration.

He died to bring you abundant life. Is that what you've been living?

No. I'd spent my life trying to prove I was worth loving. That spoke only of lack.

All that Abba has for you to enjoy can't flow into your life because all the pain you're hanging onto stops it like a dam does a river. I recalled Reverend Salem's words to me at the church and the moment of clarity that followed. My actions had blocked the blessings I sought from God.

Chase's words challenged me in ways Marine Corps boot camp never had. I had smarts enough to know the answers I needed would take time. I grabbed my journal and started writing. That always helped me sort through issues and discover deep-seated beliefs.

Fifteen minutes later my eyelids betrayed me. I hoped to interrogate Abby about her date, but sleep beckoned me. I laid my journal aside, turned off the television, and drifted off to sleep.

The moment I heard the report of gunfire, I dove off my horse. When I hit the ground, I rolled and searched for cover. A small boulder next to a scrubby bush looked promising. I crawled over to it and scrunched my body as best I could behind the rock, then scanned the surrounding area for the shooter. The open prairie terrain offered only tall grasses as hiding places. No sign of a shooter in front of me or to my left or right flank. Where were my fellow Marines? Wait…Marines on the prairie?

Had I imagined the sound? A small herd of antelope grazed about thirty yards to the east. The shot and my subsequent reaction should have sent them scurrying. I must have been downwind of them or my scent alone would have spooked them.

I turned over on my back and checked out my six. Nothing behind me.

That's when I noticed it—a bullet hole in my desert camo jacket.

I've been shot? But I don't feel a thing.

I ripped open my uniform and found a direct shot to my heart. A splotch of blood the size of a quarter colored my white undershirt. I should be dead. How could I be anything but, having taken a bullet direct to the heart. Maybe I was. Yet blood continued to slowly pulse from the bullet hole. That wouldn't be happening if I was dead. This scenario certainly didn't fit my idea of heaven or hell. I couldn't be dead.

I watched, paralyzed, as the patch of blood expanded with each beat of my heart.

Yet I didn't feel anything.

I didn't feel a thing.

Not a thing.

I bolted up in bed.

Not *this* nightmare. Not again.

Three times in less than two weeks I'd had this dream. Most recently had been while stranded by the blizzard. Would it never end?

Darkness reigned and the clock on the end table read 10:47. I felt as though I'd slept all night. Had Abby come back from her date and I missed it? I gazed at her bed in the dim light of the room. Empty.

I threw back the bed covers, grabbed my robe from the bathroom, and walked to the lobby for a cup of coffee. It was mid-brew. I sat and waited. The caffeine would keep me awake, but that was okay. I wanted to be awake when Abby got back from her date.

Papa—I'd taken to calling God that since the blizzard—You provided an amazing miracle during that blizzard. You showed me my father's verbal abuse had been like a bullet to my heart and that I had grown oblivious of the pain his words inflicted. You also showed me that until I dealt with that pain, the life I wanted would continue to bleed away. But You healed my heart when I gave up my anger. You healed that pain. Why am I still having this nightmare? What are You trying to tell me?

I listened for His answer while the coffee pot gurgled and sputtered, signaling the last of the water had been pumped through. I pulled a Styrofoam cup from the stack on the table and dumped in two packets of sugar while the last of the coffee dripped into the pot. I filled my cup, thanked the desk clerk, and made my way back to my room. Still no answer to my question.

I grabbed my journal and started writing. Then the differences in this dream hit me: I hadn't noticed the terrain or the antelope before, the bullet hole was much smaller and the blood loss way less. The two other times I'd had this dream blood had quickly saturated both my undershirt and uniform—painlessly bleeding to death. At least the blood flow had been staunched or nearly so. Significant improvement from the first time I'd had the nightmare less than two weeks ago. With all that had happened since then, it seemed more like months.

I'd fallen asleep thinking about Chase's words about blaming my father. Papa, You healed my wounded heart that night at the church, but is what Chase said true? Do I believe myself to be a victim? I want to live the abundant life You promised, but how? Do I actually play an active role in that process? If so, where do I start? I trust You to show me. Open the eyes of my understanding. Thank you, Holy Spirit, that You teach me everything I need to know.

I took a deep breath, satisfied and encouraged the Lord would lead me and reveal the answers I sought.

I turned my attention to researching the little church that had kept Abby and me safe during the blizzard and on the reverend who had pastored it. I opened the Internet on my phone, typed in *Christ Community Church Ardmore South Dakota Joshua Salem,* and waited for the results.

The news story of our recent experience topped the list. The headline read "Miracle or Hoax?" and the article included a current picture of the church. Humpf! Hoax indeed. I scanned the article while I sipped my coffee. Like all newspaper articles, it gave the facts in the first paragraph and a quote from Fire Chief Schmidt saying it "was nothing short of a miracle." But then spent another ten paragraphs refuting the miracle. I glanced at the by-line: Elizabeth Travers. Wasn't that the name of the reporter I'd seen on the TV news? Did she not realize she was calling the fire chief a liar?

Fortunately the article didn't list our names. Did that mean they'd been unable to identify us? I hoped so. I had enough to deal with without being harassed by reporters.

I went back to my search results and found an old article about the church fire and Reverend Salem's death a month later. This article included two pictures of Joshua, one taken during the fiftieth anniversary and one taken during the church's groundbreaking ceremony. Neither picture was a close-up, hindering my ability to compare them with the man I came to know at Christ Community.

Did it really matter if the reverend looked like the Joshua Salem we met? That wouldn't make the miracle any less valid. The Lord had kept us warm and well-fed in a building that had half burned and been abandoned some thirty years ago. I looked more closely at the anniversary picture. It was the closest shot of Reverend Salem. He stood at the pulpit, the stained-glass window clearly visible behind him.

I finished my coffee, then opened my Bible to read.

"The LORD is my rock, my fortress, and my savior; my God is my rock, in whom I find protection. He is my shield, the power that saves me, and my place of safety. I called on the LORD, who is worthy of praise, and he saved me from my enemies."

Thank You, Papa. You fulfilled all those roles during my fifteen years in the Marine Corps and every year since then. You showed Yourself mighty during the blizzard and I know You will continue to do so.

The clock read midnight as Abby crept in from her date with Cohen.

"You're late, young lady," I teased. I tried to maintain a serious face in the light that filtered in from the hallway.

"Gee, sis," Abby echoed my teasing tone, "you didn't tell me I had a curfew." She fumbled for the light switch.

I turned on the bedside lamp. "Is that better?"

"Yes. I should have known you'd still be awake." She moaned as she slipped off her shoes. "These are *not* walking shoes." She sat down on the bed and rubbed first one foot then the other.

"Does that mean you've been out walking with Cohen all night?"

"Not *all* night. He took me to a little Indian restaurant for tandoori chicken, then to a movie, *then* we went for a walk."

"Well, you must have been having a great time or you wouldn't have stayed out this late. I want all the juicy details." I sat up and wrapped my arms around my knees.

"What are we, eighteen-year-olds?"

I shrugged. "You're the one who said fun isn't restricted to teenagers. Besides, Chase is concerned about your heart being broken."

Abby rose from the bed. "Unzip me, will you?" She turned her back to me and I reached up and unzipped her dress. She turned back around to face me. "Every relationship carries that risk. You can't have a relationship otherwise. Even a friend can break your heart."

"Hmm. I…I guess that's true."

"Let me get ready for bed, then you can tell me about your dinner with Chase." Abby grabbed her pajamas from the drawer and padded into the bathroom.

I repositioned my pillows against the headboard and settled back to wait for her. What was there to say about my dinner with Chase? My emotional tornado had risen to an EF4, and Chase was flying a weather observation plane right through it. But if I expected details about her date with Cohen, then I'd better be willing to do the same.

Abby emerged ten minutes later. She hung her dress, shoved her pantyhose into her laundry bag, put her slip into the drawer, then climbed into bed. "So did Chase say anything about your dress? He certainly didn't have the reaction I was hoping for."

I laughed. "Oh, he did. He just didn't want you to see it. Said he didn't want to give you any fodder for teasing him."

Abby smiled like the Grinch and rubbed her hands together. "Now I have some anyway. And how did his reaction make you feel?"

Again with the psychiatrist's couch? "I have to admit, I was pretty let down when he didn't react right away." I smiled inwardly as I remembered his words. "He said, 'I thought the idea was to wow Cohen, not me.' Obviously you wowed Cohen."

"I think I wowed Cohen long before tonight. He wants to pursue a relationship."

"Holey moley!" I sat up straight. "And you said?"

"I want to hear about your date with Chase first." Abby wiggled down into the covers. Any more cozy and she'd fall asleep mid-sentence.

"Would that be considered blackmail or extortion?" I tossed a spare pillow at her. "What do you want to know?"

"All the juicy details, of course."

Abby was so much fun. Such a wonderful sister. A sister who'd been missing from my life for fifty-eight years. Why did that have to happen? I felt tears coming on. I swiped at my eyes. I hated these sudden emotional waves plaguing me. If I didn't know better, I'd have blamed it on being premenstrual. One minute happy, the next sad. Was that what grief did to you? But what was I grieving? Certainly not the loss of my father.

I heard a noise in Abby's direction and looked over. An identifiable snore escaped her mouth. Sound asleep. I smiled and shook my head. Now I'd have to wait until morning to hear her answer about Cohen. However she had answered him, she was at peace with it.

If her long night with Cohen was any indication, she'd said yes. What did I think about that? Like Chase, I didn't want to see Abby's heart get broken. *Every relationship carries that risk,* Abby's words echoed in my mind. But the depth of brokenness depended on the depth of the relationship, didn't it? And their relationship would have to navigate the distance between them once Abby returned to Great Falls. Her life was there. Cohen's was here in Scottsbluff.

Ultimately the choice was hers. I'd be there for her through the good and the bad.

Did I want to risk a broken heart by pursuing a deeper relationship with Chase? And if he broke my heart how would that impact my relationship with Abby?

I scooted down into bed, repositioned the pillows, and pulled the covers up over my shoulders. "Lord," I whispered, "protect my heart."

If you're protecting your heart, it means you expect to get hurt. No relationship can flourish under those conditions.

When I awoke at 5:05 on Saturday morning, Abby's cacophony of snores greeted me. I giggled at the revelation we had the same snore. I slipped on my workout clothes, pocketed my phone and ear buds, and made my way to the hotel exercise room. I preferred an outdoor run, and while it was actually 45 degrees out, I didn't want to risk playing pinball with the traffic. Oh, to get back to a daily routine. Nothing had been normal for the past two-and-a-half months. Could I find a routine once I got to Great Falls? Only if I made a deliberate attempt at it.

I pulled up my Bible app and scrolled to Psalm 119. Surely there'd be something in that psalm that would bring clarity to my current situation of upheaval. I put in my ear buds, warmed up, stepped onto the treadmill, and lost myself in listening to the psalm.

I was barely two minutes into my run when I heard, "Keep me from lying to myself."

The words struck me so hard I lost my step on the treadmill and nearly fell. I hit the emergency stop and regained my balance. I pulled out my phone, stopped the audio, and scrolled back through the verses to find what I'd just heard. Sure enough, it was there. "Keep me from lying to myself; give me the privilege of knowing your instructions." Why had I never noticed that before?

I slipped my phone back into my pocket and started the treadmill again. Fifty-eight years old and I'd probably been lying to myself for the last forty-eight of them. Memories came rushing in. *My mommy loved me. I don't care if my father doesn't. I'll hate him like he hates me.* And I'd done exactly that since I was ten.

Then words my father had written to me in his dying letter jogged through my mind in step with my pace on the treadmill. *Your mother's death drove me to depths of evil I never knew existed in me. ...Drove me even to murder. ...I'm so sorry for how I took my grief out on you. ...I'm proud of the woman you've become despite me.* Apparently he didn't hate me, but how was I supposed to know that when I was only ten years old and his every word and action communicated the opposite?

You blame your dad for all your problems.

Was that yet another way I was lying to myself? But surely my father had a certain level of responsibility in his emotional, verbal, and sometimes physical abuse against me.

Where did forgiveness fit into this?

That was my responsibility.

Did I blame my father for all my problems, consciously or unconsciously?

I increased the speed on the treadmill and focused on my pace and breathing instead of the thoughts bombarding me. For the next hour

I pushed myself like I was taking the Marine Corps yearly physical fitness test. After six miles, I shut off the treadmill and searched for something to wipe off the sweat. I found only paper towels. I pulled several from the dispenser on the wall and sat down on the treadmill.

Papa, show me the ways I've been lying to myself.

My precious daughter, your choices have caused the problems in your life, not your father.

I had asked God to reveal if Chase's words were true. And now He had answered. I buried my face in my hands and took several deep breaths. Papa, I'm so sorry. Please forgive me.

Of course you are forgiven. Letting go of your anger has left a big hole in your life. Now you must renew your mind and allow My love to fill that hole.

It all seemed so impossible. I took another deep breath and leaned back against the frame of the treadmill. Yes, Papa, but I'll need Your help.

You have only to ask.

I made my way back to the room. Abby was sitting up in bed reading her Bible when I entered. "Good morning. I'm surprised to see you awake already given it was after midnight when you fell asleep."

"I haven't been up long." Abby closed her Bible and set it beside her on the bed. "I fell asleep before you told me how your date with Chase went."

"Emotionally charged and awkward." I plopped down on my bed. "Other than that, it was fine."

Abby chuckled. "You have a gift for understatement. Was that all you did, go to dinner?"

"We went for a short walk afterward, but I was worn out for some reason. So we called it an early night."

"I expect that disappointed Chase." Abby rose, went to her suitcase, and pulled out a pair of blue jeans.

"If he was, he didn't say so, but he did look a bit dejected when he walked down the hall to his room. ...Now, no more stalling. How did you answer Cohen's desire to pursue a relationship?"

"I said yes." She took a deep breath. "I like him, Sally. A lot."

"And you don't have any checks in your spirit about him?"

"No, I don't, not yet anyway. But I expect you do."

"Yeah, I do." My eyebrows rose as I nodded.

"What are they?"

"He gets angry too quickly." Was the pot calling the kettle black? "But how *I* feel about him isn't important. It's not me he's interested in. Are you okay with navigating a long-distance relationship?"

"That does pose a problem, but we'll figure it out. Life is filled with adventures, and I'm going into this one with my eyes wide open. I'll know whether to end it or not without getting hurt." Abby blushed. Excitement shone from her eyes and radiated in her voice.

My sister was in love.

Chapter Nine

CHASE

"He grants a treasure of common sense to the honest. He is a shield to those who walk with integrity." Proverbs 2:7

As planned last night at dinner, Sally, Abby, and I visited Scotts Bluff National Monument, with Cohen acting as tour guide. He was quite good at it, and it gave me the opportunity not only to get acquainted with him, but also to see how Abby interacted with him.

Sally's instincts were dead on. Cohen was attracted to Abby and vice versa. I wanted to question her about her date but the opportunity to get her alone never presented itself. Given the banter between the two of them today, I surmised things went well.

After spending time in the museum, we chose to hike Saddle Rock Trail. We paired off and Abby and Cohen took the lead. I grabbed the chance to ask Sally about Abby's date.

"Did Abby say how her date went last night? By the looks of things today, I'd say pretty well."

"Yes, it did. And she—"

"Come on, Sally, out with it, unless you'd be betraying a confidence."

"I don't think I would be. …She and Cohen decided to pursue a relationship."

"You're kidding me, right?"

"No, I'm not."

"Oh boy." My stomach tensed. "Abby hasn't had a boyfriend since the last one left her standing at the altar."

"What? When did that happen?" Sally blurted, causing Abby and Cohen to look back at us. Sally stopped in her tracks and grabbed my elbow to stop me.

"Everything okay back there?" Abby hollered. They were probably about ten yards ahead of us on the trail.

"We're good." I waved my hand with an all clear, then turned to Sally. "Abby never told you?"

"No. Only said she was content to be single. Sorry I overreacted a bit." She started walking again.

"You're fine. It was some thirty years ago now. It took a long time for her to heal." I observed Abby and Cohen for a minute while Sally and I quickened our pace to catch up with them.

"I think there'll always be a bond of friendship, at the very least, with Cohen and his daughter, given the experience we shared during the blizzard. I noticed a connection developing between Abby and Cohen even then. But Abby's smart. She knows what she's doing."

"Yeah, you're right." Maybe my focus on Abby's relationship with Cohen was my way of diverting my attention away from my growing feelings for Sally. I looked down at her. Redness tinged her cheeks and nose. Was she agitated about what she'd just learned? "Are you upset or simply cold?"

"Surprised, yes. Upset, no." She cupped her hand over her nose. "But my nose is cold."

"You love being outdoors, don't you?"

"Yes." She took a deep breath and let it out as she slowly turned around taking in a full 360 view of the park. "More specifically, I love being in nature, away from the city and all its people."

"Have you always preferred that? I mean, Scottsbluff isn't a big town. Not like there's crowds to navigate through."

"I think my dislike of crowds is something I picked up in Europe. The population density is so much more than what I grew up with. And the drivers in France…wild. Like dodgem bumper cars."

We hiked the trail in silence for several minutes. Sally appeared deep in thought, and Abby and Cohen were off in a world of their own. Cohen busily pointed here and there and chattered away. Was he giving her a lesson on the flora along the trail?

"You know, Chase," Sally broke the silence. "I never gave it much thought until now, but I think I like being outdoors because that's where I feel safest."

My mouth dropped open. "Feel safe? Outdoors? Most people would say the opposite."

She shrugged. "As a kid, being outside meant I was out of reach of my father. Didn't have to worry about making him mad and lashing out at me."

"I'm sorry you grew up like that." The more I learned about her father, the more I understood her attitude toward him and why I made her nervous. Trusting men was probably a big issue for her.

"This is a revelation," she said excitedly. "Something God said to me last night…I've been living my life in protect-mode."

"You mean like you always have to protect yourself physically?"

"Not so much physically as emotionally. My father's verbal abuse happened more often and was far more damaging. For the first ten years of my life he said he loved me, but that changed overnight after my mom died."

"I can't imagine what that must have been like. It does explain your anger toward him and lack of grief about his death." Were her snarky comments a weapon of protection? Her method of proving if I could be trusted?

She scoffed and shook her head. "My belief…my need?…to protect myself has impacted my whole life without me even knowing it."

How could I respond without sounding placating? She had never openly shared anything about her life without me asking. Better to let her process her revelation without my feedback. Clearly, God was doing a work in her heart. No wonder she was caught in an emotional storm.

The rest of weekend passed pleasantly enough. Saturday night the four of us enjoyed dinner at the same steakhouse Sally and I had eaten at on Friday. Cohen seemed like a decent fellow. I watched him like a hawk—as if he was some hormonal teenager out to ravage my sister. Both were in their fifties and quite capable of making their own decisions. Abby knew she could ask me for advice anytime she wanted it. I reminded myself to back off.

On Sunday, at Cohen's invitation, we attended church with him. He admitted he hadn't been to church in years, but it was time to start back. Afterward, he invited us for lunch at his house.

"Are you sure, Cohen?" Abby asked. "I didn't take you for the type that likes to cook."

"I don't mind cooking. I can open a jar of spaghetti sauce and cook noodles."

Abby looked at me then at Sally.

"I'm fine with that," Sally said.

"Me too," I answered.

We followed him to his house, a large white home, easily three thousand square feet, with a brown brick front and three-car garage. Abby had mentioned his business was struggling, but apparently it had done well at some point in time to afford him a home that, at today's values, would easily sell for three-quarters of a mil—at least in Great Falls it would. A bit of snow remained in the yard and an abundance of red leaves from the two tall red oak trees sat atop the snow.

Cohen unlocked the front door, entered, and then tossed his keys on a black wood table beside the door. "Chase, Sally, make yourselves comfortable in the living room." He pointed to the room to our right. "Abby, would you join me in the kitchen?"

"Certainly."

They traipsed off, leaving Sally and me to lounge in the living room.

"Wow! I think my whole apartment would fit into this room and the foyer." Sally, her mouth agape, slowly turned in a circle taking in a view of the room.

A brown overstuffed couch sat along one wall, and to the left of it were two overstuffed matching chairs. A large window between the chairs offered the bright light of the afternoon sun and a view of the front yard. Across from the couch was a large gray stone fireplace, logs ready for lighting, with two leather club chairs bookending it.

Either Cohen's business made a great deal of money at one time, or he lived beyond his means. But then, who was I to say? I knew nothing of his circumstances, what his wife had contributed to the family income, or whether this home had been handed down to him just as mine had been for three generations. With the size of the oak trees out front, the home had been here for at least twenty or thirty years.

"I think I'm going to give my pilot a call and have him pick me up tomorrow, if possible." I made myself comfortable in the overstuffed chair next to the window. Sally sat in the identical one across from me. "Are you okay with that?"

"Sure."

"Do you have that cedar chest ready to go?"

"Yeah. I appreciate you taking it."

"How soon do you plan to head to Great Falls yourself?"

Sally shrugged. "I'm waiting for my father's death certificates. After that, it's just a matter of taking them to the places in town that need them."

Cohen entered the room. "Can I get you something to drink? A beer? Cup of coffee? Water?"

"Water's fine for me." I noticed a crease in Sally's brow. I imagine she didn't take kindly to the fact that Cohen had beer on hand. How did children of alcoholics feel about alcohol?

"Water for me too," Sally said.

"Coming right up." Cohen left the room.

"I know a lot of people consume alcohol without getting drunk, but it makes me uncomfortable all the same," Sally whispered.

"I understand."

Cohen quickly returned with our water then disappeared back into the kitchen. Twenty minutes later he announced lunch. We all took a seat at the table in the dining room that adjoined the kitchen, Abby prayed, and we dug into salad, spaghetti, and garlic bread.

"Cohen," Abby started the conversation, "have you seen the news about what happened at the church?"

"No, I haven't. I'm not one to watch the news. How did anyone even find out about it?"

"That's what we wondered." Abby spooned sauce over her noodles. "Apparently, some reporter learned it from the fire chief who came to the church. We saw a broadcast out of Rapid City."

"Did they mention our names?" Cohen asked.

"No. And I seriously doubt the fire chief or the police would give out that kind of information." Abby passed the sauce to Sally.

"A police report will have identifying information." Sally ladled sauce onto her spaghetti. "And that reporter struck me as tenacious. If she obtains the police report on Cohen's accident, she might get his information from that."

Cohen huffed and sat back in his chair. "I don't know if that bothers me or not. ...Why wouldn't we want them to know it was us?"

I observed the three of them as they discussed the topic. I noted confusion from Cohen, concern from Abby, and—surprise, surprise—anger from Sally.

"Because," Sally crossed her arms, "they'll invade our privacy and hound us for days. They're already questioning whether we staged it all. I was doing some research on the church myself Friday night and found a newspaper article: Miracle or Hoax?"

Cohen shook his head. "How could anyone think I staged running into the ditch during a blizzard?"

"I don't think they've thought that far." Abby wiped some spaghetti sauce from her mouth and continued. "They're questioning the miracle. Even though the fire chief reported it as such."

"I found some pictures of Reverend Salem, but none were clear enough to discern if he looked like our Reverend Salem or not. But the photo of the church taken at the fiftieth anniversary showed the stained-glass window behind the pulpit."

"And why is that important?" I asked.

Cohen leaned back in his chair and ran his fingers through his hair. "I didn't see it until the last day, but it was amazing."

"Did anyone take a picture of it, by chance?" Sally sighed, a peaceful look briefly painted her face, then her eyes went wide. "And just as importantly, in the report we saw on TV, there was no stained-glass window. Just a solid wall."

"That window mesmerized Hannah," Cohen said. "I bet she took a picture. I'll text her later and find out."

"What do you plan to do if that reporter tracks any of you down?" I plucked a piece of garlic bread from the basket.

Each one looked at me, their mouths hanging open. Sally put down her garlic bread, which she'd been ready to bite into. Silence reigned for a good thirty seconds. I hadn't meant to shock them into silence.

"I guess I'll cross that bridge if I get to it." Cohen twirled some spaghetti onto his fork and resumed eating.

"It's the press," Sally interjected. "If they choose not to believe the facts, there's little we can do about it."

"Besides, how does one prove a miracle?" Abby asked. "Doesn't it all come down to choosing to believe it or not?"

"Yes," Cohen looked at Abby, smiled, and nodded, "it does."

On the surface it seemed he was merely agreeing with Abby, but the tone of his voice carried a subtext Abby and Sally appeared to understand. Had God dealt Cohen a lesson about choices and believing during his time at the church? After all, according to what Sally and Abby told me about the weekend, Cohen had initially believed the place was a burned-out shell. Time and God proved him wrong.

"I say let's change the subject." Sally grabbed her slice of garlic bread. "Lunch is delicious. Thanks for cooking, Cohen."

"You're welcome. When do you all expect to head to Great Falls?"

"I was just telling Sally, I think I'll head back tomorrow if my pilot can get here." I turned to Abby. "Do you plan to fly back with me or drive up with Sally?"

"I'll probably stay with Sally. We never got to visit Mt. Rushmore, and she's never been. There's plenty to see between here and Great Falls, and I'm not quite ready to head home. Besides, I suspect if I wasn't with her, she'd drive straight through…with only one stop for gas." Abby pointed her finger at Sally, challenging her to disagree.

"You're right. But I'd stop to eat too." Sally chuckled. "One thing's for sure. I'll check the weather first. No more surprise blizzards."

A knock at the door interrupted our laughter at Sally's comment. Cohen excused himself from the table and made his way to the foyer.

"Good afternoon. Might you be Cohen Reed?"

We couldn't see the doorway, but the conversation was clearly audible, carried to the room by the hardwood floors and openness of the home's design.

"Yes, I am. How can I help you?"

"I'm Elizabeth Travers from the Edgemont *Chronicle*. I'd like to talk to you about your recent experience in Ardmore."

"Now is not a good time, Miss Travers. It's Sunday, a day of rest."

"The news stops for nothing."

"I'm not the news."

"Oh but you are!"

"Listen, I'm in the middle of lunch with friends. Call me tomorrow and make an appointment. How did you find me anyway?"

"A reporter never reveals her sources. But in the interest of cooperation, I pulled your information from the police accident report. There were three others with you besides the preacher. Who were they?" Travers persisted.

"I'm sorry, no. You'll just hound them the way you're hounding me right now."

"Your silence only speaks to your guilt. It was all a hoax, wasn't it, and you don't want to reveal your co-conspirators."

"Don't be ridiculous." Cohen scoffed. "No one is stupid enough to deliberately crash into a ditch and risk injury to himself or those with him."

I might have to challenge Cohen on that. Obviously that reporter was.

"I'm not saying the accident was a hoax. Just everything else that followed it."

"I see. I had an accident in the middle of a blizzard and then decided to stage a hoax miracle. Excuse me, Miss Travers, but do you realize how ignorant that makes you sound? And to the thousands of readers who read your newspaper?"

I heard the door slam shut.

Cohen returned to the dining room, head shaking, his shoulders tensed. "Did you *hear* that!"

"Yes, we did," Abby said. "You were a bit rude."

"Yeah, maybe. That bridge came much quicker than I expected it. And I'm not sure I'm ready to talk to any reporter about this. Are any of us?"

A question I was asking myself as I observed each of them around the table, the tension palpable.

Chapter Ten

SALLY

"The LORD leads with unfailing love and faithfulness." Psalm 25:10a

A flurry of activity—and not snow—filled my Monday. Staying busy would keep my mind off the fact that a reporter had tracked down Cohen, and no doubt, would eventually find the rest of us. Had any of us had the time to fully grasp what had transpired and how God had worked in each of our lives? I hadn't.

At eight that morning, Chase loaded my cedar chest into his rental car—it had a bigger trunk—and we prepared to head to the airport. Abby and I piled in and rode with Chase. Since there was no taxi service in town, Abby would keep Chase's rental car, allowing her freedom to get around town without relying on me. We drove to the region of the airport for private planes. His pilot helped load the chest, we said goodbye, and they were in the air by 10:00. A mission executed as efficiently as would any Marine Corps fire squad.

While at the airport, I received a call from Mr. Brown's receptionist letting me know the death certificates had come in the mail. Abby dropped me off at my car, then she headed off to Cohen's place. She planned to spend the day with him evaluating his business situation to see if there was any way she could help. They certainly weren't wasting any time developing their relationship.

I spent the rest of the morning dealing with the bank. I transferred my father's account into my name and arranged for the rent payments to be made to me from what was once my father's home but was now a rental. Everything went quite smoothly, which eased my emotional ups and downs. Now that I had the death certs, there was nothing else to keep me in Scottsbluff. I was ready to get on the road to Montana tomorrow. Abby, however, had said yesterday she wasn't ready to go home. How long would she want to stay?

After lunch I took a chance and drove to Jeremiah's, hoping to catch him at home. His wife answered the door.

"Hi, Claire. Is Jeremiah home? I brought a couple death certificates I thought he might need."

"He's out back. Come on in and make yerself comfortable. I'll go fetch him."

I found a seat in the living room.

"Sally. Good to see ya," Jeremiah said when he entered the room. "Claire tells me you've got Sam's death certificates."

"Yeah." I stood and pulled a manila folder from my bag. "How many do you think you need? I've already been to the bank."

"Not sure. I think most places will take a certified copy. I'll take one. If I need more, I'll let ya know."

"I'll give you six anyway. You're executor. You'll need to notify the government and such, right?" I pulled the certificates out of the folder and handed them to him. "I'll be leaving town soon, so better to have more than one."

"Yeah, reckon you're right about that." He took the certificates and laid them on a nearby desk.

"Thank you so much for taking care of my father's things. How did the auction go?"

"Very well." He nodded. "Sit down, let's visit."

What I thought would be a short visit turned into the whole afternoon. Claire pulled out photo albums and showed me pictures of them from the 1960s and '70s. Adorned in bell bottom pants, tie-dyed shirts, beads, and headbands, they looked quite the wild pair. "I remember bell-bottoms and tie-dyes. And to think, bell-bottoms are back in style. At least back then, everything wasn't so skin tight like it is now."

"No!" Jeremiah said. "Yer much too young to remember that."

"I'm fifty-eight. Granted, I was a young kid in the seventies, but I loved my bell-bottoms."

"I never would have guessed yer age." Claire chuckled. "Just never thought about it even though I remember the day they adopted you. Let me show ya some pictures from yer parents' wedding." She turned one page at a time and searched the pages for the pictures she sought. "Here!"

I followed her finger as she pointed to several photos. "I've never seen my father look that happy." A bittersweetness settled in my stomach. I loved seeing the pictures of my parents in happier days, but they also dredged up the what-if and why thoughts I wanted to avoid.

"Of course he was happy," Jeremiah said. "He was a different man then. He loved your mother deeply."

"I don't think he ever recovered from her death." Claire sighed. "Such a pity. We tried to help him, but he refused to be consoled."

"Too much pride." Jeremiah squeezed my hand and nodded at me, his eyebrows raised. Was he telling me I had too much pride as well.

As the afternoon progressed they each shared memories of my adoptive parents, including pictures of me the first week of my adoption. When it was time to prepare supper, I helped Claire in the kitchen, and we enjoyed a meal of fried chicken, mashed potatoes, cream gravy, and garden fresh corn on the cob.

"Claire, that was scrumptious. I haven't had such tasty chicken in ages, but I think it's time for me to go." I rose from the table. "Thank you both for sharing your memories with me."

"You sit yerself back down. We haven't had dessert or talked about yer biological parents." Jeremiah shook his index finger in a sit-down motion.

I complied. "Claire, make my piece of dessert small. I filled up on supper."

She dashed off to the kitchen as quickly as her age allowed her and returned with three dessert plates of chocolate cake.

I took a small bite. "So, Jeremiah, my biological parents?"

"Yes, George and Christine Leonard. Didn't know much of Christine, or even that they had three kids, leastwise, not till I read the article in the newspaper about their accident. I did business with George. Got my chicken feed and garden seeds from him. I'd see Christine in the store now and then."

"What kind of man was he?" I asked.

"A real decent sort. Church-goin' fella, I think. He ran a clean store, with fair prices, and was always visitin' with the customers."

I had hoped to gain more information than this but was grateful for it all the same. "How about you, Claire, did you know Christine at all?"

"No, I'm afraid not."

"What happened to the store after they died?"

"It got purchased by someone else here in town." Jeremiah took a bite of cake and swilled it down with a swallow of coffee.

What had happened to the money paid for the store? Was there a bank account or trust fund of some kind collecting dividends that none of us knew about? "Do you know what happened to the money from the sale?"

"I reckon it paid off any loan he had on the building and inventory." Jeremiah's eyebrows scrunched together. "I think I see where yer goin'. Surely, if there was any estate left behind, the orphanage people would have been informed of it."

"You'd think so. I'll give my lawyer a call tomorrow and add that to his list of things he's doing for me." I rose from the table once more. "Now, I think it really is time for me to be off. Thank you for the delicious meal and all your help."

They walked me to the front door. "When ya headed home?" Jeremiah opened the door.

"I'll be spending the next couple of months in Great Falls to celebrate the holidays with Abby and Chase. I'll head back to Kansas City some time after the New Year."

"If you come through here on yer way home, be sure and stop ta see us. You've got our phone number, right?" Claire pulled my jacket from their front closet and handed it to me.

"Yes, I do." I gave each of them a long hug, then made my way out to the car.

Why had life panned out the way it had? The father I grew up with was nothing like what Jeremiah and Claire described. And what about the memories Ellen Randall shared with me about my mother? As my mother's best friend, Ellen had been Mom's confidante. Ellen had dropped the bombshell about us having a brother and about my father's ultimatum of one or none in adopting a child. Now I had the added question of whether my biological parents left anything behind for us.

How different would my life have been if that drunk driver hadn't killed the Leonards? The irony of my adoptive father becoming an alcoholic after Mom's death wasn't lost on me. But thinking about what might have been wouldn't help me move forward now. I shoved the thoughts away and contemplated the two priorities on my to-do list for the coming months: determine the next chapter God had for my life, and find my orphaned brother.

Papa, what's *Your* next chapter for me?

You're my warrior daughter. You claimed an inheritance far more precious than material wealth. Now discover its depth and embrace it.

Reverend Salem had spoken those very words to me. Had it been a prophecy? Papa, I know that part of that precious inheritance is a deeper relationship with You and discovering I had a twin sister. But relationships...not my forte.

I could count on one hand the people in my life I trusted. How did I plumb their depths, let alone embrace them?

No pressure.

"So how was your day?" I asked Abby as I climbed into bed. She had just returned from another dinner date with Cohen.

"It was very nice. Cohen and I spent the day brainstorming some options for his business. Like a lot of businesses, COVID had its negative impact. How about you? Did you get the death certificates all situated?" Abby stepped out of her shoes, grabbed her pajamas, then took a seat on the foot of her bed.

"I did. All the financial stuff is taken care of, and I took several certificates to Jeremiah. Had a wonderful visit with him and Claire. And a scrumptious dinner of fried chicken." I rubbed my stomach. "We also looked through photo albums. They showed me wedding photos of my adoptive parents. I've never seen my father look that happy."

"And what'd you think about that?"

"Well, I…I struggled to believe it. After Mom died, his behavior did an about-face. I didn't know how to deal with that. In one day he went from telling me he loved me to you're not my daughter."

"And it's been almost impossible for you to trust people ever since, hasn't it?" Abby pressed her lips together and raised her eyebrows at me, challenging me to disagree. "You think on that while I change into my pajamas." She headed to the bathroom.

I threw off the covers, got up, and paced, choking back the growls pressing at my throat. My body broke out in a sweat.

Trust.

Lately, that word flew at me from all sides. But Chase pierced my spirit with the truth when he said I blamed my father for everything. For the first time, I recognized my childhood had dogged my whole adulthood. When I joined the Corps I put my father behind me, refused to think about him. I determined I would make the kind of life I wanted. And though I had succeeded to a degree, that trauma impacted every decision I made. Time for change.

Thankfully, Abby's ten-minute nightly bedtime prep gave me the time I needed to calm down. I crawled back into bed, Abby none the wiser about my mini-meltdown.

A long yawn escaped Abby's mouth when she exited the bathroom. "Didn't Jeremiah mention he knew the Leonards?"

"He did. We talked about them too." I hoped my voice didn't sound as shaky as it felt. I cleared my throat.

"Anything that might help us find Robert?" She hung up her suit coat, pants, and dress shirt, pulled down the bed covers, and sat.

"Probably not. But there is something I want to check into. They owned a feedstore. Jeremiah said it was sold after the accident. But that made me think about any assets they might have willed to us. I think tomorrow I'll give Mark a call and see if it's possible for him to look into it. Otherwise, I think I'm ready to head to Great Falls. Are you?"

Abby drew in a deep slow breath and let it out just as slowly. "Not really."

"Is that because of Cohen?"

"Partly." She slipped under the covers. "That reporter called him today. He set up an appointment to talk with her on Thursday. He asked if I'd be with him."

"Why? Does the idea of an interview intimidate him?"

"Yes. Wouldn't it you? Who knows what she'll ask or whether she'll try to twist his words."

"You've got a point. Will you tell her you were there too?" I hadn't yet made up my mind about revealing myself. I had nothing to prove to this reporter and didn't want to be hounded by her.

"I wanted to ask you about that. After he made the appointment, Cohen and I discussed whether or not to reveal everyone's names. Where do you stand?"

"I haven't fully decided yet, but at this point, I don't want her to know. And you?"

"I nursed his injury. If I reveal myself, I can attest to the fact that he was injured and that it was healed."

"Another good point." I nodded as I spoke. "Give her evidence she can't refute."

"Oh, she can still refute it. No pictures of the bruising or X-rays, so it's only our word. Really, Sally, no matter how we look at this, it still boils down to what people choose to believe."

"Totally." I pulled my knees up. "So how much longer do you want stay here?"

"I'd like to stay another couple of weeks, but I spoke with Emily earlier today and she's scrambling to prepare for her wedding and trying to run *Cattle & Cowboy*. She needs me home."

"When's the wedding?"

"Christmas Eve."

"*This* Christmas Eve? But they only got engaged in August. I remember Emily telling me the day she and Four picked me up from the hospital after my rattlesnake bite." Four, christened Chase the Fourth, was Emily's brother.

"Neither of them saw a need for a long engagement."

"Can't Leslie step in?" I straightened my legs and scooted to the edge of the bed. Leslie was Chase's oldest. She and her husband, Jake, had been real thorns in my side during my four weeks at the ranch. A thorn in my side? Maybe I did have a gift for understatement. Jake had tried to kill me. "Wasn't managing the magazine her job before all that mess with Jake?"

"Yes, but he's been found competent to stand trial, and Leslie's an emotional mess."

"That's understandable. He tried to kill me, and now he has to face the consequences. What woman wouldn't be a wreck facing that?"

"Leslie has never handled not getting her own way very well. If he goes to prison, I can't imagine how she might react." Abby reached out and clasped my hands. "Will you come to Great Falls during the trial? Having you there will help me."

I smiled. "Of course, I'll come, but Jake admitted to trying to kill me. Why would there be a trial?"

"All I know is the evaluation said he's competent to stand. So I'm assuming there'll be one. Will you stay until it's over? I see a very rocky road ahead."

"I'll stay as long as you want me to. Now, how long do you want to stay here?"

"Are you okay with another week, long enough to do the interview with that reporter?"

Abby spent three weeks in Kansas City helping me and another week to deal with my father's death. How could I not agree to her request?

"After all you've done for me, of course. Besides, Cohen's not so bad after all, and I'm the one who encouraged your relationship with him. I'd be an idiot to try and get in the way of it."

Chapter Eleven

SALLY

"He leads the humble in doing right, teaching
them his way." Psalm 25:9

On the intervening days, I decided to join Abby and Cohen's interview with Elizabeth Travers. This reporter had accused us of perpetrating a hoax, and I wanted a handle on how desperate she was to prove her theory and how we might prove her wrong.

Meanwhile, Abby spent nearly every waking hour with Cohen. She was falling hard and falling fast.

The evening before the interview Abby's niece Emily called while we lounged in the room watching TV.

"Hi, Emily, how are you?"

I muted the TV so it wouldn't interfere with their conversation. A long silence ensued as Abby listened. She wet her lips repeatedly and squeezed her brows together. Not good news then.

"Have you talked with Leslie?" Abby asked.

Another long silence.

"Okay, hon. Sally and I already planned to leave this Friday and should arrive home Saturday evening. Don't fret. It'll all work out. Love you." Abby clicked off the call.

"Problems?"

"A kitchen fire gutted the venue they had booked for the wedding reception. She's overwhelmed and desperate for me to be back at work."

Abby's reluctance painted her face.

Sweet Emily, Chase's youngest, was running *Cattle & Cowboy* magazine, doing both Abby's job and Leslie's in their absence. Plus planning her wedding. Was it any wonder she was frantic.

The next day dawned rather stormy. At least it was only rain and not snow. We drove to Cohen's at eleven for an early lunch and to pray about Travers' interview at one thirty.

"I toyed with the idea of staying longer, Cohen, but I'm needed at home." Abby began the conversation after we finished praying. She took a seat on the living room couch. "Emily is managing my job at the magazine plus trying to put together her wedding."

"When is it?" Cohen sat beside her.

"Christmas Eve. Will you be my plus one?" She twined her fingers with Cohen's.

"I'd like that, but it would mean leaving Hannah alone on Christmas, and I don't want to do that."

"Bring her with you. She's more than welcome. Does she like horses?"

"She loves horses."

"Then she'll love being at the ranch. She can spend time with Pete and Gabe, Chase's twenty-four-year-old twins; they train our horses. There's plenty of room for you both to stay at the ranch or my house. Please think about it." Abby shifted closer to Cohen and smiled to encourage him.

I turned a bit warm with embarrassment watching them. Did they forget I was in the room?

"Okay. I'll talk to her about it when she comes home for Thanksgiving." Cohen ran the back of his index finger down Abby's cheek, then stood and paced the room, glancing at his watch. "Sally, I still don't understand why you want to be here without actually participating."

"I want to get a better feel for this reporter's intentions. On the TV report she gave, she sounded adamant that what happened was a hoax. Who knows what she'll say or do to make her point."

"Okay." He shrugged and looked at his watch again. "Sure wish she'd get here. She's ten minutes late."

"Maybe she won't show up at all and then—" Abby attempted, but a knock at the door told us otherwise. We looked at each other for a moment.

I took a deep breath. "Show time."

Together Abby and Cohen strode to the door, and I darted to the kitchen where I would spend the duration eavesdropping.

"Good afternoon, Mr. Reed. I apologize for being late. The storm delayed the cameraman from getting here."

"Cameraman? No, no, you never said anything about being filmed," Cohen protested.

"I assumed you'd know that was part of the interview."

I wanted to peek around the kitchen corner that led to the front hallway to observe the expression on Travers' face, but I dared not. I strained my ears instead.

"Newspaper reporters don't need cameramen," Abby said.

"Oh, but I'm no longer a newspaper reporter. The TV station in Rapid City hired me shortly after I took this story to them."

I realized then we were dealing with a very determined, possibly manipulative, woman. Maybe she saw this story as her doorway to a spot with the national news.

"Sir, I drove three hours to get down here. It's not a live interview, only recorded." Must have been the cameraman.

"I'm sorry for the misunderstanding," Travers said, her tone sweet and syrupy rather than apologetic.

"I'm not happy about this," Cohen said. "But come on in."

"Thank you," Miss Travers said.

I listened to shuffling footsteps and the clunking of camera gear as they entered the house.

"May I look around the house for what offers the best background and lighting?" Travers asked.

"No!" Cohen spouted, the pitch of his voice rising with his nerves.

I chanced a peek. Cohen stood with his hand held out toward the living room.

"I won't have my privacy invaded any more than necessary. The living room has more light than any room in the house. It will have to do."

Miss Travers pursed her lips, and I noted a shadow of displeasure cross her face. She stepped into the living room. I quietly slipped over to the other side of the kitchen nearest the living room.

"Can you make this work, Jerry?"

"Not a problem at all. The lighting is great. And the fireplace will make a homey background. We just need to rearrange the chairs."

I heard some grunting as someone moved furniture and Travers' staccato voice directing the placement of said furniture. "Can we light the fire? It'll add atmosphere."

"In case you hadn't noticed, it's not a gas fireplace. It could be a good thirty minutes before we'd have a fire that adds *atmosphere*." From Cohen's tone, I surmised he regretted agreeing to the interview.

"Oh. Well...okay." Her tone carried annoyance. "Jerry, let's get a sound check and then get started."

Again more shuffling, throat clearing, a three-second countdown, then a moment of silence.

"I'm here today in Scottsbluff, Nebraska, with Mr. Cohen Reed and Ms. Abby Reynolds. Mr. Reed, tell our listeners about the *miracle* you experienced two weekends ago at Christ Community Church, near Ardmore, South Dakota."

"You can't appreciate the true miracle unless I start at the beginning."

"Then I guess you'd better tell us," Miss Travers said, her tone pleasant this time.

Undoubtedly her reporter persona. Oh for a fly's eye view of her face.

"I had a conference to attend in Rapid City. My daughter and I were headed up when we got caught by the blizzard. Because of bad visibility I missed a curve in the highway and ran into the ditch. Thankfully, the church was nearby and we took shelter there.

"Man, what a shambles! A fire had charred one side of the church. The four windows on that side were boarded over. Dead leaves and a pile of snow occupied a corner. I thought we might actually stay warmer in my car."

"When did Miss Reynolds show up?"

"She was there when my daughter and I arrived."

Cohen continued his story, piece by piece, including how he had placed his hand on the pot belly stove to prove its coldness and then ten minutes later, toppling into a pew as I poured steaming coffee into his cup.

"I'm sorry, who's Sally?" Miss Travers interrupted.

"Sally Clark, my sister," Abby said.

None of us realized that in telling the story, we would reveal who else had been stranded there.

"So your sister was the fourth person, not counting the reverend?"

"Yes, that's right." Abby confirmed.

"And what brought you to the church, Miss Reynolds?"

"The blizzard, of course."

I clamped my lips shut to stifle a chuckle. I doubt that was the answer Travers wanted. I was grateful for our morning prayers and that we had prayed with Cohen during lunch. We wanted and needed the presence of Holy Spirit to guide Abby's and Cohen's words.

"Where were you headed?"

"To Rapid City to see Mt. Rushmore. The storm took us by surprise. We hadn't checked the weather before we left Scottsbluff, but who expects a blizzard in mid-October?"

Travers chuckled. "I think that storm caught a lot of us by surprise. What did you think of the church, Miss Reynolds?"

"A beautiful pristine little country church. Reverend Salem greeted us when we arrived. He was busy bringing in wood for the stove, but the electricity was on when we arrived. The storm knocked it out later that same day, but we stayed quite comfortable and well fed the whole three-and-half days we were there."

"Wait. Mr. Reed, you described the church as a burned wreck. And you, Miss Reynolds, as beautiful and pristine. It's one or the other," Travers insisted. "Which one of you is lying."

"Lying?" Abby exclaimed. "Neither of us, Miss Travers. That's the miracle. My sister and I had faith for God to provide us shelter from the storm. And He did."

"And their faith opened my eyes to the miracle," Cohen added.

"More like fooled you, you mean," Travers gibed. "You want me to believe you stayed warm and fed in that dilapidated church?"

"Yes!" Cohen almost yelled the word.

"You have the words of Chief Schmidt," Abby said. "The place was warm and we fed his crew a hot breakfast. Are you calling *him* a liar?"

Great shot, Abby, right across Travers' bow! Had that been inspired by the Holy Spirit? I'd have to ask her when they were done.

"Like I said, I touched that stove twice without getting burned. I didn't warm up enough to take off my overcoat until after Sally poured me that steaming cup of coffee. I touched the stove after that and nearly burned myself. Every moment after that I began to see what they did, right down to the amazing stained-glass window behind the pulpit."

"Stained-glass window? There's nothing but a solid wall behind the pulpit. This is nothing but a hoax," Travers protested.

A moment of silence ensued. How would Abby or Cohen respond? Or had the tidbit about the window left them all speechless? But I realized that was our ace in the hole. I had the newspaper article with the picture of Joshua at the pulpit with the window clearly visible behind him. I nearly bolted into the living room to confront Travers, but the Holy Spirit restrained me. The time for that was for another day.

"I don't think you fully realize what you're saying, Ms. Travers." Abby's voice rang with confidence. "Who in their right mind would stage an accident that could potentially seriously injure themselves, during a blizzard when help might be out of reach?"

"I'm not saying the accident was a hoax," Travers responded.

"So I had an accident, and then got the brilliant idea to stage a hoax at the nearby deserted building while snow piled up all around us."

A longer period of silence followed Cohen's statement. I wished I could see Travers' face. Was truth dawning or was she too blinded by atheistic beliefs?

"We know what we experienced, Ms. Travers," Cohen broke the silence. "A warm and comfortable church that kept us safe and quite cared for during the storm. *That* is the miracle. I didn't agree to this interview so you could sit here and accuse us of lying. What you choose to believe is up to you. We're done."

"But—"

"I said we're done."

"All clear," Abby hollered from the foyer after closing the door behind Elizabeth Travers and her cameraman.

I joined her and Cohen in the hallway.

"We need to pray for that reporter. I honestly think she fully intends to prove what happened was all a hoax." Abby led the way into the living room where she and Cohen proceeded to move a club chair back into place. "Wouldn't you agree, Cohen?"

"Yes, do I." Cohen stood up from moving the chair. "But she's obviously not thinking straight. She says me running into the ditch wasn't planned, but then she leaps to the conclusion that everything that followed was. How could anyone plan being stranded in a blizzard after crashing into a ditch in the middle of nowhere?" Cohen moved the second club chair back into place by the hearth.

"I saw the camera guy flash her several angry looks." Abby dropped into said club chair. "I think she manipulated him into showing up just like she tried to manipulate the whole interview."

"You guys did great. I only wish I could have seen Travers' face when you told her it was up to her to choose what she believed, Cohen." I took a seat on the hearth.

"Thanks, but I'm sorry about inadvertently mentioning you, Sally." He took a seat in the matching club chair.

"Don't worry about it."

Cohen had learned a lot while being stranded. His power to choose being primary. I picked up an entirely different vibe from him now than at the church. Maybe I had misjudged him. I noticed Abby smiling, a lost-in-thought glint in her eye. "Earth to Abby." I waved my hand in front of her. "What are you thinking about?"

"We've changed—in different ways—because of our experience. We don't need to prove anything to anyone, so don't let her push you into it. Either of you." Abby pointed first at me, then at Cohen. "We related our experience. Whether Miss Travers accepts or rejects it is her problem, not ours."

I thought about that for a moment and realized the truth of Abby's words. I also realized I'd fallen for Travers' ploy. I'd spent my whole life trying to prove myself to others. It had become an unconscious behavior. Time for change.

"I agree, Abby, we don't need to prove anything. That comment about Chief Schmidt and accusing him of lying was brilliant. How did you ever think of that?"

Abby shook her head. "That just came tumbling out. Holy Spirit giving me the words I needed for the moment."

"Wish I could have seen Travers' face. At any rate, if she forces our hand about proof, we've got what we need." I looked at Abby, then Cohen, my eyes wide and eyebrows raised.

"What do you mean?" Cohen asked.

"The stained-glass window. She said there wasn't one. And remember, Abby, I mentioned it missing in that report she gave?"

"Yeah, I'd forgotten that. But how does that help us?"

"I found a picture online that shows Joshua standing in front of that window."

"Then why didn't you interrupt the interview to tell us that?" Cohen sounded a tad angry.

"I wanted to, but I sensed Holy Spirit restraining me, saying that was for another time."

We stood looking at each other. Cohen stood stock still and his mouth dropped open. I heard Abby suck in a quick breath. What were they thinking?

"It looks like our miracle is about to become someone else's." A wide smile slowly worked its way across Abby's lips.

That night as Abby and I prepared for bed I decided to ask her about how she'd changed. I hadn't noticed anything, but I also didn't know her that well just yet. "Abby, earlier today you said we've all changed. I can see that change in myself, but how have you changed? How has Cohen?"

"You remember how keyed up and anxious Cohen was? His anger level? It's gone. He's found God's peace. He even told me he's okay with closing down his business if that's what needs to happen." She pulled down the covers and got into bed.

"I'm sure having you here has helped him." I climbed into bed and sat crossed legged. "What changes have you noted in yourself?"

"A greater faith and trust in God. You?"

"The same. I'm more tuned into His voice, too, in a way I've never been. I'm really excited about the coming months in Great Falls and opening the next chapter of my life."

"Do you know what that might include?" Abby had her eyebrows raised and sly smile on her lips. I suspected she hoped I'd say a relationship with Chase.

"Aside from maybe starting on that book I've always wanted to write, I'm not sure."

"God will show you." She reached up and turned out the bedside lamp. "Good night."

"Good night. Sleep tight." I made myself comfortable then turned my mind to what God had done since August. Papa, what did I do to deserve this avalanche of blessings?

I bless My children because I love them, not because they've done something to deserve it. You've been seeking change in your life all year. I brought you that opportunity, though you didn't recognize it as such when it showed up in your mail. Remember, initially you threw away that letter from Kandell Law Offices. It was your choice to respond to it, and your choice to claim the inheritance. You can turn away from My blessings just as easily as you can embrace them.

Wow, Papa, that's amazing.

Calling God Father always put me in mind of my earthly father, and I wanted and needed some separation from that. Papa fit well, bringing me a sense of calm and love, like being wrapped securely in God's arms.

Trepidation about my next question trembled in my stomach. I suspected what the answer would be and anticipated its heaviness on my spirit. Papa, have I turned away from Your blessings at other times in my life?

Oh, yes, as have all of human kind, so don't get down on yourself about it. Learn from this experience, ponder the things that come your way, and make more informed choices about them.

Yes, Papa.

Time to look forward to the abundant life Jesus promised instead of always looking at my problems.

Chapter Twelve
SALLY

"Be still in the presence of the LORD, and wait
patiently for him to act." Psalm 37:7a

A week had passed since my father's death certificates arrived. I spent that week talking with the police about what they knew of George and Christine Leonard. Nothing I could find helped me determine if they had willed anything to their children. I had one last meeting with Mr. Brown and left the job in his capable hands. If I kept adding to his list of things to do, I might as well hire him as my full-time lawyer.

Now, with sunny but cold weather, Abby and I headed to Mt. Rushmore once more—this time I avoided the scenic route. We would spend today playing tourist, then drive the other eight-and-a-half hours to Great Falls tomorrow. We drove the first hour and a half to Rapid City in silence. Thoughts of the time ahead in Great Falls occupied my mind. I suspected Cohen occupied Abby's. Time for some conversation.

"Abby, I don't think I ever told you, but before I flew to Montana to spend my four weeks at the ranch, my friend Jen Maxwell spoke a verse over me. Isaiah 61:7, 'Instead of shame and dishonor, you will enjoy a double share of honor. You will possess a double portion of prosperity in your land, and everlasting joy will be yours.' Coming into a deeper relationship with God and finding you is the best *double portion* I could ever receive."

"Sally, that's a wonderful Scripture and promise. Remember it whenever you start to question your circumstances. Two inheritances inside of three months certainly qualifies as a double portion of prosperity. But you've also received two new families."

"*Two* new families? How's that?"

"The Reynolds clan and our brother when we find him."

"You're right! I sure hope Mark can get the adoption records opened." Abby had accepted me without reservation. All but one of Chase's six kids welcomed me with open arms. Chase himself? That took longer. Four weeks to be exact, at the end of which he confessed he might be falling in love with me. Remembering those words made my stomach flip and my heart race.

"Speaking of things you never told me reminded me of something," Abby said. "I secretly recorded our interview with Miss Travers."

"Ooo, Abby, you sly dog." I flashed her a grin. "What prompted you to do that?"

"All the manipulative things I noticed in her behavior. I thought it would be a good idea to have a recording of my own in case she tries to twist our words…and I'm almost positive she'll do just that."

"I wholeheartedly agree. From the moment I saw her on the first news report something in my gut didn't sit well about her."

"Me too. I'm certain we haven't heard the last of her."

"For now, let's focus on having a good time over the holidays. How does your family usually spend them?"

"We gather at the ranch for a big meal and family time." Abby repositioned herself to face me. "Everyone pitches in cooking the Thanksgiving meal. We play cards or board games after eating. I'm not quite sure what Christmas will be like. Normally it's the same as Thanksgiving except for the added time of opening presents together. But with Emily and Matt's wedding on Christmas Eve, I don't know how that will impact Christmas day."

A glistening red Corvette startled me as it zoomed by in the left lane. I guess if I owned a fancy sports car, I'd want to speed down the highway too. It struck me that with nearly $200,000 now sitting in my bank account I could buy a sports car if I wanted. But I'd rather give toward disaster relief or supporting a missionary. Maybe I could do both.

"I'm praying Cohen and Hannah will come for the wedding and Christmas. I expect I can have our pilot fly down and get them to save them the drive time and gas money."

"Must be really nice having your own private plane and pilot."

"With the traveling I do for work, it is. And now it's something you can enjoy."

I glanced at Abby who sat smiling at me. I had inherited a one-third portion of the ranch profits, but I didn't realize that entitled me to the use of the company jet. "I can use the company plane if I want?"

"I don't see why not. You own a percentage of the ranch business and part of *Cattle & Cowboy*. More importantly, as my sister, you're part of the family."

"But—"

"No buts about it. As the father of the prodigal son told the older son 'all that is mine is yours.' You are part of the Reynolds family now, and you can enjoy all that we enjoy."

"Abby, I…thank you. So few people have ever treated me the way you and your family does." My throat choked up.

"I'm sure Ellen Randall did. And your friends John and Jen Maxwell do. You'd probably find a few more if you stopped to think about it. That anger you've operated from all your adult life has blinded you and kept the door closed to the good things in your life. 'As a man thinketh, so is he.' Your thoughts have a tremendous impact on your life."

"So Holy Spirit has been teaching me. Guess I have plenty to contemplate while I'm in Great Falls."

I'd spent plenty of time considering Abby's and Chase's advice about creating the life I wanted. The idea galvanized me. What did I envision God's abundant life included for me?

Chapter Thirteen
CHASE

"Wise choices will watch over you. Understanding
will keep you safe." Proverbs 2:11

Sally's choice to stay at the ranch for the duration of the holidays pleased me. I had Rita prepare the same bedroom Sally used when she was at the ranch before. I moved her cedar chest from the garage to her room, then went downstairs to the kitchen.

"Rita, Sally will love you for fixing beef stew for dinner. I think it's her favorite meal." I inhaled deeply and enjoyed the enticing aroma of the beef and veggies simmering in the slow cooker. "It'll be good to have Abby home again too."

"Yes, it will. I'm baking her favorite dessert."

"Thank you. You're an angel in disguise." I gave her a quick kiss on her cheek. "Sally's here until after New Year's. An extra mouth to cook for, but don't let her being here interrupt your normal routine. I'll see to any special needs she might have."

"Okay, Chase. Thank you. I'm sure it'll all be fine. She was no bother before. She won't be now. So, out of my kitchen. I've got Abby's apple pie to bake." She shooed me away with her hands. Rita had been our cook and housekeeper for nearly twenty years, and a real mainstay since my wife's death.

I walked to my office at the south end of the house. What could I keep myself busy with for the next six hours of waiting for Sally and

105

Abby's arrival? I dealt with my email, then sauntered out to the ranch office in the barn to brief the boys.

"Hey, Pop," Peter greeted me.

"What's up?" Gabe asked.

"Nothing special. I expect Sally will be working with you while she's here. Maybe we need to find her a steady chore to occupy her time." But then again, maybe she already knew how she planned to stay busy.

"Pop, you look as nervous as a mouse who just spotted the barn cat." Peter laughed. "What gives?"

"Don't be ridiculous. I'm fine. I don't want Sally to get bored, that's all."

"Yeah, right." Peter elbowed Gabe who stood nearby.

"And that means?" I cleared my throat.

"It's okay," Gabe chimed in. "We know you like her. We're good with that."

I nodded. "Good to know." I tried to act nonchalant, but their words brought me some relief.

"She more than proved herself to us during the trail drive. The horses sure have missed her," Gabe said. "What time are she and Aunt Abby due in?"

"Around dinner time. Rita's got beef stew cooking and is baking an apple pie…or two."

"Apple pie! It's been ages since we've had any. I'll eat a whole one myself." Gabe laughed then quickly sobered. "You know, Pop, I never realized what a calming influence Aunt Abby is to Emily and Leslie. They've been driving me crazy."

"They're both in stressful situations right now, so tread lightly," I advised. "Besides, how can they be driving you crazy? Neither one lives or works here on the ranch."

"They've been calling us twice a day with 'I need a favor,'" Gabe explained.

"Hm. Okay. I'll talk to them."

"Daddy!" The shriek came from down the corridor. It was Leslie, my oldest, and the only one who insisted on calling me daddy.

"Speak of the devil. I'm glad she's here for you and not me," Peter whispered, then turned back to the work on his desk.

I turned and made my way through the barn. When I met up with Leslie, she held some papers in her left hand, tears stained her cheeks, and her eyes were red and puffy. That seemed her permanent condition since Jake had been arrested for attempting to murder Sally nearly two months ago. I still struggled to fathom that my son-in-law had done that. And now, as I looked at the distraught Leslie, I wondered where the strong, confident woman I knew had disappeared to?

"Leslie, what's wrong?"

She fell into my arms and sobbed. "What am I going do? Jake is filing for divorce."

"He's what?" I grasped her shoulders and held her at arm's length.

She held the papers out toward me. "He's filing for divorce."

I took the papers and began reading. Sure enough, he'd filed a petition for divorce. "I can't believe the courts found him competent to stand trial. Nothing he's done since August has made sense."

"Daddy, I'm beginning to doubt I ever really knew the man. He's so changed."

"Come on up to the house. I'll make some of that tea you like so well, and we'll talk." We walked to the house. I deposited the sobbing Leslie in the great room in a chair by the fireplace then went to the kitchen.

"Rita, have you got some of that special tea Leslie likes so well? I need to make her a cup." I filled the teakettle, then lit a burner and placed it on the stove to boil.

"The tea's in the cupboard to your right. Is everything all right? She only asks for sassafras when she's upset."

"Jake filed for divorce. Her mom always knew how to handle these kinds of situations." I sighed. "I'm glad Abby will be home tonight. She'll know what to do."

"I'm sure you'll do just fine." Rita went back to rolling pie dough.

I noticed two pie pans on the counter and a large bowl of sliced fresh apples. "Glad to see you're making two pies. Gabe's threatened to eat a whole one himself."

"I'll box his ears if he tries."

I smiled, knowing Rita would hug him instead. Before long I had Leslie's tea ready and made my way back to the great room. She had calmed down considerably.

"Here you go, hon." I handed her the cup.

"Thank you, Daddy." She took the cup and started blowing to cool the tea a bit. "I guess this is for the best."

"You resigned yourself to that rather fast."

"Oh, I've seen it coming. I've thought about it myself."

"After the scene I witnessed between you two during the trail drive…well, I think divorce is the answer in this situation."

"Daddy, you can't be serious. Divorce goes against God's principles."

"That's true. But the way he grabbed you that night, I bet it left bruises on your arms. Be honest."

"Yes, it did."

"Has he ever hit you?"

"No, but it's not the first time he left bruises on my arms."

"I don't think it's Jake that's changed. I think you've come to your senses about who he truly is. You're safer without him. He had us all fooled." Jake had been a competent ranch manager, but he had a streak of meanness that reared its head now and then among the ranch hands. And apparently against Leslie as well.

"Daddy, how could I have been so blind? I feel so foolish." She started crying again.

I pulled her up from the chair and held her tight. "You'll get through this."

Chapter Fourteen

SALLY

"Do not remember the rebellious sins of my youth.
Remember me in the light of your unfailing love,
for you are merciful, O LORD." Psalm 25:7

That evening when I pulled onto the blacktop driveway that led to Chase's ranch, an audible sigh escaped Abby's lips.

"I expect you're glad to be home. Well, almost home," I said.

"Almost home?"

"This is Chase's house, not yours."

"I grew up here. It's more home than the house I own."

I parked the car to the side of the ancestral log and granite home. It didn't appear as massive to me now as it had the first time I arrived three months ago. I sat staring at it, remembering how much of an unwanted stranger I'd been that first night.

"Everybody! This is Ms. Sally Clark," Four had yelled. Some of the gathered crowd smiled but mostly they sat there, mouths agape, acting as though I was a grizzly poised to attack. The group chattered about my amazing resemblance to Abby. That was before I knew she was my twin. I learned that the next day when I saw a portrait of what I thought was me, hanging in their dining room. My mug of coffee dropped from my hand, the mug shattering and coffee splashing across the hardwood floor.

"I meant to tell you…" was all Chase said. For a good week I wrestled with the idea that I was the illegitimate child of the man who'd left me the inheritance that brought me to the ranch.

So much happened during the four weeks the inheritance required I spend at the ranch—a cattle stampede, a rattlesnake bite, arrested for theft and jailed, then bailed out. At that point, I didn't want the inheritance because it looked as though it was going to cost me my life. Chase and Abby managed to change my mind. The day before I was due to return home to Kansas City, Jake, Chase's son-in-law, tried to kill me. The will stipulated that when I died, my share of the magazine would go to Leslie, Jake's wife. He wasn't willing to wait.

All that seemed a lifetime ago.

In the intervening weeks since then, my father had died and I'd been stranded by a blizzard in southwest South Dakota. All this had wrought minor and major changes in my life, in me, and in my perspective on life.

Now I was here not as an unwanted stranger but as a welcomed family member. All because of a chance meeting between me and Chase's parents in Paris, France, of all places.

My car door opening of what seemed its own accord startled me from my thoughts.

"Welcome home." Chase stood there, tall and unwavering, the same as he'd done that first time I arrived at the ranch.

I looked over at the passenger seat, but Abby wasn't there. "Where's Abby?"

"She walked through the door ten minutes ago. Have you been sitting here since you pulled up?"

"Yeah. Been thinking about that first night I arrived and everything that's happened since." I climbed out and walked to the trunk to get my suitcases. Chase started to lift two cases from the trunk.

"Those are Abby's. Just leave them. I'll drive her into town later."

He grabbed mine, and together we walked into the house, Chase pulling my suitcases behind him.

I smelled beef the moment I walked through the door. "That smells scrumptious. I don't know about Abby, but I'm famished."

110

"I'll carry your cases upstairs later. You're in the same room as before." Chase left the luggage sitting at the foot of the stairs. "Rita's had stew simmering in the Crock-Pot all day. It's ready whenever you are."

"I'm ready." We walked to the dining room. Abby, Pete, and Gabe were seated at the table. "Let's eat!"

Rita carried the pot to the sideboard, then lifted a napkin from a nearby basket, revealing a loaf of sliced homemade bread. We all helped ourselves and took a seat, including Rita. Chase said a prayer then I chowed down.

"Rita, this is delicious. Thank you," I said.

She smiled her *you're welcome*.

"So, did you drive all day without stopping?" Chase teased.

"It took some convincing on my part," Abby mocked, "but she agreed to stop for lunch."

I snickered. "Some Marine habits have served me well. Chase, do you mind if I have my mail forwarded to this address? I've had the PO holding my mail since I went to Scottsbluff nearly three weeks ago."

"Of course not. We get our mail at a PO box. We can deal with it in the morning."

Our banter continued for more than an hour as we enjoyed a leisurely dinner and dessert.

Strangely, I felt like I was home.

As the days past, I reestablished my daily early morning run, which went a long way in calming my emotions. That run was my quiet time with God. I continued to seek His guidance on the next chapter in my life.

My recent inheritances had left me financially independent, but I had no intention of living a life of leisure. God had a purpose for me; the Bible told me that much. That I was still on this side of the grass meant He had more for me to do. Only one definite answer had revealed itself: don't start a publishing business. My desire to write grew stronger.

Abby returned to her work at *Cattle & Cowboy,* and Chase played tour guide, showing me several favorite tourist spots and the falls for which the city was named. They were beautiful and I marveled that I stood at the headwaters of the same Missouri River that cut through Kansas City. Here in Great Falls the river enticed me with its sparkling shallow water, the exact opposite of the deep Big Muddy I knew. The vast openness of the surrounding terrain exuded peace. No traffic noise. No high-rises. No pollution. Just fresh air, the sounds of nature, and lots of sunshine.

Montana had cast her spell on me. I knew then and there, I'd return to Kansas City only long enough to pack up and move to Great Falls. I decided to announce that news during the Thanksgiving meal.

After a few days playing tourist, I shifted to working with Pete and Gabe. While they trained the two-year-old horses, I kept the others exercised. I took Sandy, a magnificent palomino, out for a daily ride, another factor that relieved the chaos swirling in my mind.

But it was all a stalling tactic.

When I rose from bed on a chilly November Monday morning, the cedar chest and the *For Sally when she turns eighteen* box residing in the chest stared me in the face as it had each morning and night since I arrived in Great Falls. Every day I battled the thought of *what would my life had been like if.* The moment it raised its ugly head, I took control of it like the Bible said to do. Just as I had done while in the Middle East and all throughout my Marine Corps career. Much of my military discipline seemed to disappear the day I first stepped foot on the Reynolds' ranch. That day I felt like an ant invading a royal palace.

I knew starting a publishing company wasn't the right direction, but I hadn't pressed for other answers. Mostly, I thought about Chase. Veteran's Day was only four days away, daring me to reclaim command over my life. I'd answer that dare. I'd been drifting down the river of indecision too long.

To cement my commitment, I went for my usual morning run. When I stepped outside the cold air slapped me in the face. I ignored it. At least I wouldn't have to spend the entirety of my run in the dark.

Daylight Saving Time had said goodbye, and Standard Time reigned the day once again. I turned my focus to God, and His peace entered my soul.

Three miles and a shower later, I lifted Mom's box out of the chest and took it over to the bed. "Papa, bring only happy memories as I go through these items. Please keep my grief to a minimum."

Pictures and numbered envelopes filled the box. I sifted through the photos. Most were of me at various ages, and each had an explanation on the back. *Sally's first steps. Sally's first birthday*—with chocolate cake smeared all over my face. *Sally's first owie—accompanied by tears and a bloody knee.* I chuckled at that one. *Sally's first day of kindergarten.* And I wore a dress! Back then girls were required to wear dresses to school. Oh how I rejoiced the day I finally got to wear pants to school in the tenth grade.

A knock at the open door interrupted my memories.

I looked over. "Come on in, Chase."

"Good morning." He took a couple steps into the room. "Rita's about to clean up from breakfast. If you want to eat, you'd best come down or you'll have to forage for yourself."

"Oh, wow. I lost track of time looking at all this."

Chase stepped over to the bed and picked up one of the pictures. "What's this?"

"Look on the back."

He flipped the picture over. "Sally's first owie." He looked up from the picture, smiling, and then scanned the items strewn across my bed. "Is this what was in that white box you found?"

"Yes. I finally mustered the courage to open it."

Chase picked up one of the numbered envelopes. "What's in these?"

I shrugged. "Not sure. I haven't opened any of them yet. I assume they're letters my mom's written. I'm also assuming she numbered them with the intent that I open them in that order."

"How many are there?" Chase replaced the envelope he'd taken.

I flicked to the last of them in the box and pulled it up far enough to reveal its number. "Twenty-one."

"I reckon that'll keep you busy today. A hardy breakfast will help. Come on. You can enjoy the last of the eggs, sausage, and hash browns."

I rose from the bed and we walked down to the dining room. Pete and Gabe still sat enjoying their coffee.

"Morning, Pete, Gabe," I said when I entered the room. I headed for the sideboard and began lifting the lids off the chafing dishes. Chase wasn't kidding when he said *the last of*. I scraped the three dishes clean of food and sat down to eat. Chase had already poured me a cup of coffee.

"How does Rita manage to cook exactly enough every day?" I asked.

"Years of practice," Chase proclaimed.

"Pete, Gabe, can you do without me today?" I looked at them.

"We don't have enough to keep ourselves busy, so you'll be fine," Peter said. "Sandy might miss you though."

"She'll get her exercise. I'm just waiting for the temp to warm up." I turned to Chase. "Would you like to join me today? Maybe we can do a sunset ride like we did during the trail drive?"

"I'd like that."

My day was planned, and my sunset ride would provide the tranquility I would probably need after reading my mother's letters.

After breakfast, I pulled a pile of tissues from the box in the bathroom in preparation of the tears I anticipated with reading Mom's letters and ambled back to my room.

I got comfy on the bed and grabbed letter #1.

Dearest Sally,

In this box you'll find twenty-one letters. The first eighteen you can read now. Save the others for the corresponding birthday. I debated having your father give you these on your birthday each year but I don't trust him to remember. He's a good man and loves you in his own way, but…

I considered giving the letters and the box to Ellen Randall but felt it was a burden too far beyond what I have already asked of her.

Had I been eighteen and reading this, I would have wondered what burden Mom was talking about. Now I surmised it to be the secret of my brother and sister she wanted to adopt but wasn't allowed. I went back to the letter.

It broke my heart when I first received my diagnosis. I wasn't worried about dying—I'd be with Jesus. But I dreaded not being there to raise you. Every girl needs her mother. I asked Ellen to look after you once I'm gone. She said yes, and I know she'll keep her word. I can only hope you didn't give her a hard time.

I rolled my eyes. Ellen did great. Me? not so much.

Letters one through ten contain pictures and memories of each of those years of your life. Eleven through twenty-one are my dreams for you for each year and for the woman you'll become.

Remember always, I love you dearly and look forward to our reunion in heaven.

Love, Mom

The rest of letter held memories of my first year. When I took my first step, my first word, my first tooth. I smiled as I read, enjoying the journey of learning about myself and the things Mom and I did together. I pulled out the pictures in the envelope. One was of my father pulling me in a wagon. He had a big smile on his face. If only...there was that thought again. If only he'd given me this box when I turned eighteen maybe I wouldn't have spent the next forty years being so angry at him. We might actually have had a decent relationship instead of being estranged.

I sighed, pushed those thoughts aside, and grabbed the next letter.

I read through the first ten then broke for lunch. Chase was at the table when I came down.

"You must be enjoying those letters. You have a big smile on your face instead of swollen teary eyes."

"You expected me to cry all morning?"

"Well..."

"That's okay. I expected tears too." I grabbed a plate from the table and filled it with a sloppy joe, chips, and a dill pickle, then took a seat. "I've only read ten of them. They're her memories of my ten years with her. Eleven through twenty-one are her dreams for me for each of those years. Those might be tougher to read."

"That was a very thoughtful thing for her to do."

"Yes, she brought those memories back to me. I'd lost them in my battle to survive my father's verbal abuse. And they've given me some peace and more of a sense of belonging."

"That's great. You said you were tired of being lonely." Chase reached over and squeezed my hand.

I smiled wanly. We finished our lunch in silence and I went back to my room to finish reading the letters. What would they hold and would I find that my life was, at least in part, what she dreamed for me? She had probably dreamt of my wedding, and later, spoiling her grandchildren. What mom doesn't? I only hoped who I had become wasn't a disappointment to her.

When I got to letter twenty-one, I found a picture. This surprised me. Letters eleven to twenty didn't have any. And I didn't expect any. They were letters of my future. How could they contain pictures?

I pulled out the picture and examined it closely. A woman held two infants, and a little boy stood beside her, one little hand fisting her skirt. I flipped it over, praying Mom had captioned this like she had all the others in the box.

Mrs. Lowenfeld holding Sally and Abby, Robert standing beside her.
Realization dawned. I ripped the letter from the envelope.

Happy 21st birthday, my sweet pea!

I imagine by now you are nearing your college graduation. What have you become? A teacher, perhaps? Though as often as you pretended to solve mysteries, I expect you have aspirations of being a detective. You can do anything you set your mind to, sweetheart. Seek the Lord's guidance in all you do and don't rely on your own understanding.

I think by now you are ready for something I've kept secret from you all these years. I thought it was for the best. But now, as I face death, I question all my decisions except the one to adopt you.

At this point in her letter, tears stained the paper.

When your father and I visited the orphanage, I fell in love with you the moment I saw you…and your twin sister. Yes, you have an identical twin. And a brother three years older than you. I wanted to adopt the three of you, but your father said no. It was one or none.

Mrs. Lowenfeld and I grew up together. She saw my dilemma. She felt my heartache. I begged her to take a picture of the three of you so that one day you could track each other down. I pray every day you will meet one day, and I will continue to beseech the Lord once I am in heaven that He will bring you three together once more.

I am so sorry, darling. I hope you can find it in your heart to forgive me for keeping this secret.

Love always,

Mom

The answer to her prayer neared fruition. Only finding Robert was left. I dropped the letter on the bed and ran from my room, hollering for Chase as I dashed downstairs.

Chapter Fifteen

CHASE

"For wisdom will enter your heart, and knowledge
will fill you with joy." Proverbs 2:10

"C hase!" I heard Sally yell. Her voice held excitement yet was somewhat frantic too. I exited the corral and headed toward her voice. "Chase!"

I caught her by the shoulders as she ran up to me. "What is it? What's wrong?" I searched her eyes, her face, for an inkling of the problem.

"Look." She held out a picture to me. "It's me, Abby, and Robert."

Taking the picture from her hand, I recognized Abby immediately. I'd seen enough baby pictures of her over the years to know. I flipped the picture over. "Lowenfeld? Wasn't that the name of the orphanage?"

"Yeah, it was. My mom and Mrs. Lowenfeld grew up together, and Mom convinced her to take this picture."

"It's nice you have it, but what good does it do you?" I handed the picture back.

Sally looked down at the photo then up at me. Wrinkles creased her brow. She heaved a sigh. "I guess none. For a moment...I thought... blast!" She closed her eyes and tipped her head back. I watched her shoulders rise and drop with each breath, disappointment filling the air with each exhale.

"Listen, why don't you get the picture blown up, poster size maybe, and framed," I suggested.

"That's a great idea. Thanks. I'll have two made, one for me, one for Abby. Sorry I bothered you." She turned and trudged back to the house, her shoulders slumped.

What must she be feeling right now? Her excitement at having found the picture was obvious, and I had quenched that excitement like a bucket of water on a blazing campfire. I glanced at my watch, nearly four. Sunset was only an hour away. "Sally," I hollered and jogged toward her. She stopped and looked back. "It's time for our ride."

She looked at her watch. "But it's barely four o' clock."

"Yes, and the sun will set around five. ...Go put your picture in a safe place and grab your jacket. I'll saddle the horses."

When Sally returned to the barn, she had changed from her tennis shoes to her cowboy boots and had donned her Stetson as well. Her dejection had disappeared. Sandy whinnied at Sally's approach.

"Sandy's glad to see you."

"She always is, aren't you, girl?" Sally rubbed Sandy's cheek.

We mounted and headed north from the ranch across the vast prairie to an ideal spot to observe the sunset.

"Did you get all of your mother's letters read?"

"Yeah, I did. Her dreams for me were to be a teacher, but she also recognized I might lean toward police work. Apparently I played detective a lot." Sally chuckled. "I'd forgotten that, and being an MP isn't something I aimed for. That's just where the Marines put me."

"Did she explain the picture of you three?"

"Yes. It was her way of righting the wrong...of not adopting all three of us. She wanted us to find each other. I can't help wondering how differently my life might have been if my father had given me that box when I turned eighteen. Or for that matter, if my mom had chosen to give me those letters each year on my birthday instead. And please don't give me a lecture on what ifs."

"Hadn't planned on it. But I'm available if you ever want to talk." We rode the remaining distance in what was for me an uncomfortable silence. I tried to ease my discomfort with the beauty of the golden prairie as far as the eye could see and the silhouette of the distant mountains.

The sunset lacked vibrancy, but maybe the tranquility of the settling of another day would bring some peace to Sally's turmoil. "We'd better head back while we still have the twilight."

Sally's silence as we rode weighed heavily on me, but I knew she had to ruminate on recent events. She needed to find resolution for herself, with God's help, not me riding in to rescue her. Instead, I would challenge her to think about her options.

"Are you going to tell Abby about the picture you found or surprise her with a poster?"

"Haven't considered it yet, but I like the idea of surprising her." She seesawed a bit in the saddle, a smile on her face. "A Christmas gift would be perfect, if I can contain my excitement that long. I'll drive into town tomorrow and get the project started." Her upbeat tone belied the downheartedness I sensed from her.

"What's it been...a month or more since Pendrake Publishing turned down your offer to buy them out? Do you think your co-workers would have accepted you becoming their boss?"

"I actually never thought about that. But I think they would have been okay."

"Have you given anymore thought to what you'll do now?"

"Aren't you a fountain of questions tonight! I know one thing: I'd like things to calm down. My time in the Middle East had fewer bombshells."

"I doubt that. The difference is you knew how to deal with those bombs. Those of late, you don't."

"Good point." Sally sighed. "One day at time. I'm seeking the Lord for answers."

"Best thing you can do. At least there hasn't been any more hoopla on the news about the church."

"Maybe there has been, but we've missed seeing it. I'll give Abby a call when we get to the house and see if she's heard anything from Cohen. She's invited him as her plus one to Emily's wedding. Did she tell you?"

"No, she didn't. How serious has their relationship gotten? Do you know?"

"I have my suspicions, but that's a question you should ask her not me." Sally raised her eyebrows in that Groucho Marx manner that declared you'll-be-surprised. "Race ya back. Hyah!"

And she was off.

I pushed my Stetson on tighter, heeled Molly into a gallop, and raced after her. Sandy was our fastest horse, but mine was in the top three. I'd give it a good try.

Minutes later our horses were neck and neck as we galloped into the barn yard. Sally whooped, hollered, and laughed the whole way. I had observed an openness and freedom like this in Sally only one other time, and that was when we were out for a ride. For her, being on the back of a horse was like the thrill I felt as I watched each of my children step into the destiny God had for them as adults. Truly, Sally belonged here. Had she come to realize that yet?

"I win! ...Whoa, Sandy." Sally reined in her horse. "What a rush!"

I reined in Molly right beside her, adding to the cloud of dust Sandy had created. "Better than your morning run?"

Sally laughed. "In its own way, yes. I think Sandy enjoyed it too." She leaned forward and patted Sandy's neck then dismounted.

I dismounted and we led the horses into the barn. "Dinner will be ready soon. We'd better get these horses brushed down fast or Rita might have our hides for dinner."

Sally chuckled, then grabbed my arm, leaned up and kissed my cheek.

"What was that for?"

"Nothing special." She grinned. "Just thanks."

More evidence of her softened heart. God was indeed doing a work in her.

Chapter Sixteen

SALLY

"Trust in the LORD and do good. Then you will live
safely in the land and prosper." Psalm 37:3

The race home from my sunset ride with Chase exhilarated me. I felt alive and more in tune with who God created me to be. I no longer felt like a victim of my circumstances. Rather, like Abby said weeks ago, I had begun to see I could create the life I wanted no matter what circumstances came my way. Hadn't I already done that when I went to college at the age of thirty-three for a degree in English? Hadn't I made the choice to work at Pendrake Publishing in Kansas City, and most recently the choice to quit Pendrake and come to Montana? Adrenaline pulsed through me as I realized the power I had over my own life through the choices I made.

After supper, I retreated to my room to call Abby.

"Hi, Sally. How're things going at the ranch?"

"Just fine. Chase and I had a tranquil sunset ride. He mentioned he hadn't heard any news about the miracle. Has Cohen mentioned anything about the interview with Travers?"

"No, but it's only been about two weeks since the interview. Maybe they're saving it for Thanksgiving week. You know, things to be thankful for."

"Maybe, but somehow I don't think that's the angle that reporter is looking for. By the way, be prepared for Chase to ask you about your relationship with Cohen." I grabbed my pajamas from the hook on the closet door and tossed them onto the bed.

"Why?"

"I mentioned you invited him as your plus one to the wedding, and he asked me how serious your relationship was. I told him to ask you."

Abby laughed. "Thanks for the forewarning. Cohen and I FaceTime every night."

"Wow, sounds more serious than I thought. Is he coming for the wedding?"

"I don't know yet. Hannah gets home from school Thanksgiving week. He isn't sure she'll want to come and feels uncomfortable about leaving her alone on Christmas. You and I aren't strangers to them, but spending Christmas with the whole Reynolds clan might be over-whelming to him."

"I think Hannah would love it." I put my phone on speaker and laid it on the table by the chair. I sat, tugged off my boots, then wiggled and splayed my toes.

"Enough about that. It's Veteran's Day on Thursday. Let me take you to lunch to say thank you for your service."

"That sounds fun, thank you. I can tell you all about what was in that box my mom set aside for me."

"Anything exciting?"

"Oh yeah," I said but didn't offer anything more.

"Sally, you need to write mystery stories."

"Why's that?"

"Because you're so good at leaving people with cliffhangers. You're actually going to make me wait two more days before you tell me what you found?"

"I'll offer you a tidbit. She wrote me twenty-one letters. And before you ask, yes, I've read them all."

We chatted a while longer then said good night.

I changed into my PJs, and by nine I tumbled into bed happy and tired and slept a solid seven hours.

I awoke the next morning with one task in mind: find a photo studio that could scan, enlarge, and create a poster-sized print of the picture of Abby, me, and Robert.

With the temperature at 22 degrees, I skipped my run. I showered, ate breakfast—the dining room was empty—and made my way out to the barn office.

"Hey, guys, what's on today's agenda?" The office was too full for me to enter. Four, Michael, Pete, Gabe—Chase's sons—and Chase sat shoulder to shoulder. Their faces looked as though I'd caught them smoking behind the barn. "A big pow-wow, huh? Sorry to interrupt."

"No problem. We were discussing the candidates for ranch manager. We have four applicants coming in for interviews," Chase said.

"Who's been handling Jake's duties since he got arrested?"

"Four and I have been," Michael answered. "It's worked but isn't ideal. Winter is slow at the ranch. A great time to break in a new employee."

"I'm headed into town. Won't be here for lunch, but I'll be back by dinner; I'll let Rita know. Good luck with the interviews." I waved, left them to their business, and got about mine. My cell phone rang before I got back to the house.

"Hi, Jen, long time no talk. How's life?" My friend and former co-worker at Pendrake Publishing had, like me, quit her editorial position at Pendrake.

"It's great, Sally. I wish I'd gone freelance years ago. I've got coaching and editing clients. All the business I need and want. How's Montana?"

I continued my walk to the house. "Already dipping into the twenties at night, but in the forties during the day. It *is* only November. Who knows what Old Man Winter will bring when he makes his official appearance." Montana's weather had been a pleasant surprise up to this point. The temps warmed nicely during the day but cooled down at night. Oddly it didn't feel as cold as Missouri. Chase had explained that was typical of a semi-arid climate.

"I wasn't actually wondering about the weather," Jen said. "I was hinting about the cowboy that comes with the place. I know you probably don't want to talk about that, so I'll get to the reason I called."

"Hmm, sounds like bad news." I reached my car and clicked the key to unlock the door.

"I think it's good, but you might not. John made partner and we've decided to stay in Kansas City."

"That's great news, Jen. Why would I think otherwise?"

"Because we talked about starting our own publishing business, but you didn't want to stay in KC to do it."

"The Lord's told me starting a publishing business isn't the right thing to do. Has He given you any leading about that?"

"Yeah. That was my next piece of news. You've just confirmed God's message to me. I can't tell you how much relief that brings me. I didn't want to let you down."

"Jen, you aren't letting me down. I don't want us to go down a path God doesn't have for us. You and John are doing what you want to do, what you're passionate about, what God has called you to do. That's wonderful. You're living the life you've chosen."

"I'm so glad to hear you say that. I'm really lovin' what I'm doing."

"Will you edit my first novel? Even editors need an editor."

Jen laughed. "I'd be glad to. How soon will you have it done?"

I scoffed. "The million-dollar question. Instead I'll give you my million-dollar news. I've decided to move to Great Falls."

"Wow! How soon?"

"After the new year. I'm going to enjoy the holidays and look around for a house. Is everything okay at my apartment? Are you keeping my plants watered?"

"Yeah, things are fine." Jen sounded a bit sad. "I'm missing you already. I'll have to throw a moving-away party for you."

We chatted about a couple of her clients and the stories they'd written, then hung up. I went back to the barn office to talk to Chase. "Sorry to interrupt again, guys."

"Don't worry about it. What do you need?" Chase asked.

"Is there a place in town I can buy a classy bottle of champagne and have it sent somewhere?"

Chase shook his head. "We don't do alcohol, not even at our big soirées."

"Why not buy online?" Michael asked.

"Because nothing says personal like a hand-written note. I can't do that ordering online."

"I'm sure there's a wine or liquor store in town. What do you need champagne for?" Chase asked.

"A friend in Kansas City just made partner in the law firm he works for. I want to send it as a congratulations."

"Four was headed into town to pick up some salt licks, but why don't I do it? You can come with me, and we'll find that champagne you need and do whatever else you planned." Chase turned to Four. "Does that suit you?"

"Suits me fine."

"Great. But, Sally, maybe you want time to yourself for your errands?" Chase asked.

"Not necessarily. I'm down with having a chauffeur. But I thought you had interviews to conduct."

"That's tomorrow. Let's go." Chase stood and slipped his hand down my back in a motion to usher me out of the barn. The warmth of his hand permeated my jacket, warming me in the process. I liked his hand being there, yet it also left me feeling uncomfortable. Men were only gentlemen when they wanted a "favor" from me. His hand dropped away as we walked the aisle leading outside.

"Do you want to be there to celebrate with them? I can have Steve fly you there if you like."

"Goodness no. Jen, didn't mention any planned celebration. I don't know any of the lawyers John works with. I'd be totally out of place."

"John? The lawyer who was here in August to get you out of jail?"

"The very same. You know, I can smile and half-laugh about that now, but in my book, having me arrested for theft was one of the worst decisions you ever made."

Chase chuckled. "I've made plenty of bad decisions, but you're right about that one."

Chapter Seventeen

SALLY

"O LORD, oppose those who oppose me. Fight
those who fight against me." Psalm 35:1

I quietly looked out the window while Chase drove us into town.
The landscape had changed considerably since I was here in sum-
mer, but every season held its own beauty. The empty wheat fields
seemed to call out to me. I leaned toward the window, preferring to be
galloping across those fields on Sandy.

"You'd rather be on a horse, wouldn't you?" Chase asked.

I glanced over at him and then back out the window. "Definitely. I
was thinking about how it must have looked back in pioneer days. No
fences, no telephone poles, no electric wires, whether it was forested or
always a prairie."

"You belong here, you know. What's to keep you in Kansas City?"

"Nothing. But I seem to remember, I told you during the trail drive
I planned to leave KC."

"I'd forgotten that. Well, you need to move here."

I smiled at Chase and left him to wonder. Would I be able to hold
out till Thanksgiving, telling him I planned to do just that? I half felt
telling him would jinx things. No bombshells had dropped since learning about how my biological parents died, but I was on high alert.

I reminded myself daily that God told me to discover the depth of
my inheritance and embrace it. I sought to know God better by read-

ing the Bible more often and journaling my conversations with Him. I chanced being playful with Chase last night, thinking that would open a door to know him better. Living in the same house with the Reynolds family for two months certainly ought to help me grow closer to them. But the vision of myself as an ant at the royal palace still invaded my thoughts. When it did, I took command of it and cast it away.

If I was ever going to create the life I truly wanted, I had to start by seeing myself the way God saw me and imagining myself already being the person I wanted to be. But I hadn't quite captured that vision yet.

When we arrived in town, cars crammed the streets, and the sidewalks bustled with people and pets. Chase had to park two blocks from the photo studio. We climbed out of the pickup and headed down the sidewalk.

"Who's calling Abby's name?" Chase placed his hand on my forearm, stopped, and looked around.

I hadn't heard anything, but who notices a voice unless they're calling your name? We were barely five feet from the pickup.

Chase shook his head, apparently having not spotted anyone he knew, and we continued to the photo shop.

"Miss Reynolds!"

This time I heard the voice too. A woman wildly waved both arms while dodging the traffic on her way across the street.

"It's that reporter from Rapid City," I whispered to Chase. "How did she find us?" I briefly entertained the idea of playing dumb. I could easily deny I wasn't Abby Reynolds, but to deny I wasn't her twin would be tough.

Miss Travers was a bit winded by the time she caught up to us. "I'm so glad I spotted you, Miss Reynolds."

"Abby Reynolds is my sister," Chase said. "And I can tell you unequivocally, this is not her."

"Mr. Reynolds, it's nice to meet you. I'm Elizabeth Travers." She stared at me as she spoke. "You've cut your hair since I last saw you, but why deny who you are?"

"Because I'm not Abby Reynolds. I'm Sally Clark. What do you want, Miss Travers? Mr. Reynolds and I have business to attend to." I stayed calm but spoke with all the authority I had once used as an MP.

"Sally Clark? You're trying to prank me." Travers laughed. "I'm here hoping for a follow-up interview with you."

"Then why didn't you simply pick up the phone and call?" Chase asked. "Did you think showing up in person would convince Abby to say yes?"

I looked up at Chase who looked down at Travers. His height and girth exuded power. A frown creased his lips and wrinkles lined his brow. Looked like Travers left a bad taste in his mouth the way she had me.

"Call and make an appointment like any respectable person would do." Chase crooked his hand around my elbow and we continued down the street.

"But why can't I make an appointment now?" she called after us.

I looked back at her. "Because you need to talk to Abby to do that."

As we made our way to the photography shop, I glanced back several times. I expected to find her following us, but she wasn't. Either that or she was acting all spy-like and concealing herself. Once inside the shop, I turned to Chase. "Something about that woman sets alarms ringing in my spirit."

"Me too. She's a determined little filly, that's for sure."

"Little filly? She's a barracuda in a clown fish disguise."

"Can I help you?" the girl at the counter asked.

"Yes, but give me a minute please." I pulled my cell phone from my back pocket and dialed Abby.

"Hi, Sally."

"Abby, that reporter's here in town. She wants a follow-up interview."

"What? How do you know?"

"Because she just approached me on the street, thinking I was you. Chase told her to call and make an appointment."

"Okay, if she calls, I'll talk to her."

"No, make an appointment and *we'll* talk to her. This girl's out for blood. Even Chase got a bad feeling about her." I held the phone out to Chase who leaned toward it.

"Sally's right, Abby. You two need to present a united front with any follow-ups."

"All right. I'll let you know if I hear from her. Bye."

I ended the call and pocketed my phone.

"Why do the media find it so hard to believe miracles happen?" Chase shook his head.

I dropped my chin and raised my eyebrows at him.

"Yeah, I know. Obvious answer. Because most don't believe in God."

"Did I hear you say miracle?" the store clerk said.

"Yes, you did." I stepped to the counter. I guessed the girl to be about sixteen or seventeen. "I've got a picture I'd like enlarged into a poster. Can you do that?"

"Probably. I'll have to check for sure with my dad." She stepped to a curtained doorway and stuck her head around the curtain. "Hey, Dad. I need you out here a minute."

She returned to the counter and I pulled the envelope with the picture in it from my purse.

"My mom homeschools me and we've been talking about Jesus' miracles. What miracle are you talking about?"

"Bailey, don't be nosy," her dad said from the curtained doorway. "How can I help you folks?"

But Bailey's enthusiasm delighted me. "I'd like this picture made into a poster." I handed him the photo.

"Are you talking movie poster size?" he asked.

"No, one step down from that, I'd say."

"Do you want it framed as well?"

"Yes, definitely. Can you do it and still keep the picture clarity?"

"Yes, ma'am. I can have it ready next week sometime."

"I need two, but I'd like to see the picture first once you enlarge it."

"Not a problem." He took my details.

"And Bailey, I'll tell you all about my miracle when I come to get my posters." I smiled and nodded at her.

"Thanks!"

When we left the shop and headed to get my bottle of champagne, I spotted Miss Travers across the street watching us. She made no attempt to hide herself even though she saw me looking at her.

"Don't look now but Ms. Travers is following us," I told Chase.

Chase looked around all the same. A scowl appeared on his face once he spotted her. "I'd say she's one step away from stalking you. Can you keep an eye on her without her knowing we're doing just that?"

"Of course I can. Who knew I'd be using my military police skills when I was fifty-eight years old? Go figure."

We walked several blocks to the liquor store, Travers never far behind.

I explained to the clerk what I needed and arranged for it to be shipped to Jen and John at their home address. "I'd like to include this personal note with it." I pulled out the card I'd pre-written from my purse and handed it to the clerk. "How long before this gets there?"

"We can have it overnighted if you like."

I stopped to think. If I was going to splurge and buy champagne, I might as well go whole hog. I wanted Jen and John to know how special they were to me. "Yes, overnight it."

He rang up the bill and I swiped my debit card in the card reader. "Do you have a back door out of here?"

He gave me a quizzical look. "Yes we do. It's only for deliveries."

"We've got a TV reporter stalking us. If we can go out the back, we can lose her."

"Someone's stalking you? I'd call the police." He busied himself with the necessary paperwork needed for shipping the champagne. "If you could fill this out please. Will you want to insure it?"

"Yes." While I filled out the form, I mulled over the idea of calling the police. That seemed a bit extreme. For now, I'd make my point by outsmarting her. "I hate to call the police. She's not dangerous, just persistent. Could you please let us out the back?"

He took the shipping form from me and perused it. "Everything looks good, Miss Clark." He looked at me then at Chase and shrugged. "Why not? Follow me."

The clerk led us through the store and unlocked the back door.

"Thanks. Nothing like a little cloak and dagger to add excitement to your day." Chase shook the clerk's hand.

"Yeah, come back any time. Good luck, and thanks for your business." He stepped back into the shop and set the lock.

"Which way to the truck?" I asked.

"South…to the right. Why?"

"We need to head in a direction away from the truck."

"How 'bout we stop by Abby's office and see if she wants to join us for lunch?" Chase held his arm out to the left of where we stood, and we headed north down the alley.

"That's a great idea."

"It's too far to walk, so we need to get back to the truck."

"Let's go down one more alley. If we exit here, Travers might spot us again."

We crossed the street and walked the length of another alley to the next street. Then zigzagged our way back to the truck. "I certainly hope Abby and I won't have to be looking over our shoulders from now on. I wonder if all reporters are as rude as that woman."

"The few I know aren't." Chase unlocked the truck and opened the door for me. I slid in then scoured the area for Travers. Our stealthy exit from the liquor store had been successful.

"This is a nice surprise," Abby said when we entered her office.

"We were in town on business and thought you'd like to come to lunch with us." Chase turned his Stetson around in his hands. Did he go anywhere without wearing it?

Abby looked at the clock on the wall. "Eleven thirty. We can beat some of the rush." She pulled open a desk drawer and took out her purse. "Did you have some place in mind already?"

"I didn't." I looked at Chase. "Suggestions?"

"What are you hungry for?"

I shrugged. "I'll defer to you and Abby. I just want something hot."

Abby's office line rang just as she stepped out from behind her desk. "I'd better get that. I've been expecting a call from our printer in Michigan."

Chase and I both nodded.

"Hello?" Abby answered. "This is Abby. And you are?"

Obviously not the call she was expecting. She punched a button and hung up the receiver.

"This is Elizabeth Travers. I'd like to talk to you some more about your supposed miracle."

Speaker phone, gotta love it.

"Now's not a good time. We could schedule a time for next week."

"Next week! I'm already here in town. You know that. I don't know why you refused to talk to me earlier today." Travers' frustration and anger bubbled through her words.

"No, Miss Travers, I didn't talk with you earlier today. You spoke with my twin sister, Sally Clark."

"Oooooooh. The sister you were with at the church?"

"Yes, but there's really nothing I can add to the interview you did with Cohen and me last month."

"But I've been to that church several times since the blizzard. It's falling apart. There's simply no way you could have stayed warm and fed for the time you were there."

"That's what makes it a miracle, Miss Travers."

"I don't believe in miracles."

"And since you've chosen what you want to believe, nothing I say— or anyone else who was there—will convince you otherwise. I suggest you interview the first responders."

"I want to interview you."

Abby moved several items on her desk to reveal a desk calendar. "I'm available next Tuesday morning at ten o' clock." She looked at me, questioning if that time was good for me. I nodded my approval.

"You have nothing sooner?"

"No, I don't. I run a business, Miss Travers."

Travers' huff at Abby's response was audible. "All right. Can your sister be there too?"

"Now you want to interview her too? ...I won't promise. I really must go. Goodbye." Abby ended the call before Travers could respond.

"What does she hope to get out of this?" Chase donned his Stetson. "Did you notice? Not a single *please* or *thank you*?"

"I've been praying for her, and the Word says you can't mock God. She'll reap what she's sowing," Abby said.

"I think she's climbing the ladder to a position as an anchor on national news." I turned and headed out of Abby's office. "She's a pain in the patootie."

Chase laughed. "Patootie! Haven't heard that word in decades." And he laughed some more.

"You're laughing now, Chase, but she may prove to be more than that," Abby said solemnly. Her words carried an ominous prophetic weight.

Veteran's Day dawned, bringing with it a heaviness as I remembered those with whom I'd served and who had died. "Heavenly Father," I whispered while lying in bed, "be with their families and comfort them. Despite the years that have passed, they are no doubt remembering them as I am."

I grabbed my Bible from the bedside table and opened to Psalms. I could always trust the Psalms to bring whatever I needed for the day, be it peace, encouragement, or guidance. David held nothing back in his communication with God. I liked that. I read for an hour, then showered, dressed, and went down for breakfast.

Cheers of "Happy Veterans Day!" greeted me when I entered the dining room. Above the sideboard a banner stating the same covered the wall. I looked at Chase, Pete, and Gabe who stood smiling at me.

"You were busy concocting this when I interrupted you in the office yesterday, weren't you?"

"Guilty," Chase said.

"But we really do have interviews to conduct all day today. So we thought we'd make breakfast special for you." Gabe pulled out a chair and motioned for me to take a seat. "We'll serve you."

"We're glad you're here," Pete said.

"Thank you so much." I gave Pete and Gabe a hug, then sat. Since the first day I'd come to the ranch, they made feel accepted when so many others saw me as an interloper. "I'm meeting Abby at her office at 12:30. She's taking me to lunch. If Rita has anything special planned for supper, I'll be full as a tick by day's end."

"There's waffles, sausage, and scrambled eggs. What would you like?" Gabe took my plate from the table and walked to the sideboard.

"Give me some of each and drizzle warm maple syrup over it all."

Chase filled everyone's cups with hot coffee. "Rita said she'd fix your favorite dessert if she can find a recipe for it. What is it?"

"Cherry pie with a scoop of ice cream on top." I looked up at Gabe when he set my plate down. "Thanks, Gabe. You guys are so sweet to do this."

"Rita can manage cherry pie just fine. She thought it might be something French since you spent so much time in Paris." Chase filled his plate and sat beside me.

"Are you particularly excited about any of your job candidates? When's the first interview?" I asked.

"Nine o' clock." Pete stabbed a sausage link on his plate. "We're agreed on two that have the greatest potential."

"Besides lunch with Aunt Abby, how are you going to spend your day?" Gabe asked.

"You know, Gabe, I think I'm going to crack open my laptop and start on that novel I've wanted to write for the last ten years but haven't gotten to."

"Excellent! What's it about?"

"The attempted murder of a Marine who receives an inheritance, snake bite and all."

Gabe and Pete had a good laugh over that. "Will we be in it?"

"Of course."

They finished breakfast then excused themselves. "See you later, Pop," they chimed then ducked out the door and headed to the barn.

"How have those two kind-hearted polite souls managed to stay single? Every girl in Great Falls must be after them."

"I think they're hoping to meet twin sisters." Chase chuckled. "Can I get you more coffee?"

"Yes, thanks."

He rose, retrieved the carafe from the sideboard, and filled both our cups, then set the carafe on the table. We sat staring at each other. The bronze flecks in his eyes seemed to flicker. No smile creased his lips, but neither did a frown. What thoughts filled his mind? "A penny for your thoughts?"

"Oh, my thoughts are worth much more than a penny," he teased.

I decided to play along. I pushed my empty plate aside and leaned over on the table, my arms crossed. "How much more?"

"Ten times."

"Wow, a whole dime. I think I can afford that. But I'll have to pay you later. I don't have any money on me at the moment."

"Then I'll guess you'll have to wait to find out."

I playfully nudged his shoulder. "You're going to make me go find a dime?"

"Hey, you're the one who offered to pay me for my thoughts. But I think you're good for a loan." He dug around in one pants pocket then the other, searching for the required coin.

"Thanks again for the special breakfast. I…I'm feeling more a part of the family each day that passes."

"I'm glad." Smiling, Chase pulled his fist from his pocket and dropped several quarters, a nickel, and two pennies on the table. But no dime.

"I guess I'll have to borrow a quarter." I picked one up and held it out to him.

His smile disappeared, and his hand wrapped around the quarter, enveloping my hand in his as he did. He laid his other arm on the back of my chair and leaned forward. His eyes locked on mine as though he was searching the depths of my soul.

Butterflies invaded my stomach.

The grandfather clock in the hallway chimed seven.

The approaching sunrise tinged the horizon.

How long would he make me wait before he answered?

"I was thinking about how much I'd like to kiss you."

My mouth dropped open.

"Does that sound too cheesy?"

I worked to recover myself. "I…no…I mean…"

"No snappy comeback? That's a first. I'll leave you to think about it." He grinned, gathered up the coins on the table and put them back in his pocket. "You can keep the quarter."

And he sauntered off to the barn.

What was I to do with *that* revelation?

I sat stunned for several minutes, working to get my head around that idea. Did I want to kiss him back? I wasn't sure, but the thought didn't bring rise to any fear.

What a kink in my day. How could I plot out my novel with Chase's words pinballing around in my head?

"Happy Veteran's Day, Sally." Rita's words pulled me out of my head.

"Thank you, Rita." I rose and helped her clear the dirty dishes. "Chase mentioned you offered to make my favorite dessert for supper tonight. Thank you. It's cherry pie with ice cream."

"Cherry pie it is."

We finished clearing the dishes and I meandered to my room. Chase's words banged around my mind like tennis shoes in the dryer. I did my best to turn my imagination to plotting my novel. I'd only been teasing when I told Gabe what it was about, but that story would write itself. All I'd have to do would be to change the names and location. Instead, maybe I could write a romance about twin brothers who fall in love with twin sisters. That sounded fun. I booted up my laptop, opened a document, and started brainstorming.

Midmorning, the photo shop called. They had the enlargement ready. I'd stop by to give my approval before meeting Abby for lunch. They could have the final framed pictures ready by next week. Would I be able to keep this surprise a secret until Christmas? Such a perfect gift for Abby. I'd stash mine in the closet so there'd be no chance she'd see it and spoil my surprise.

Then Jen called to say how delightfully surprised they were with the champagne I'd sent. We spoke for a while, then I left for my lunch with Abby, without having accomplished much toward my novel.

Over lunch, Abby and I discussed the upcoming interview with Miss Travers.

"What can she ask that she hasn't already?" I asked.

"I don't know, but I think we need to find verses from the Bible to refute her."

"She doesn't believe in God. What good will sharing verses from the Bible do?"

"She's a lost soul or so it seems. Maybe what we need to focus on is presenting the gospel to her."

Abby's statement pricked my soul. That hadn't even occurred to me. I sighed. "You're right. As Jesus taught, love your enemies and pray for those who persecute you."

We made plans to meet tomorrow morning to put it all together and pray for Miss Travers.

But it was all for nothing because when Monday rolled around she called Abby and canceled the interview. She'd been called back to Rapid City to cover some other breaking story. "She sounded very agitated at having to leave, but I'm relieved she's gone," Abby told me over the phone.

"Me too, but I have a sneaking suspicion we haven't heard the last from Miss Travers."

Chapter Eighteen

SALLY

"My problems go from bad to worse. Oh, save
me from them all!" Psalm 25:17

The days to Thanksgiving passed quickly. The Reynolds men focused on training the new ranch manager, and despite the upcoming holidays, life at the ranch and for me settled into a new routine. I filled my mornings planning my novel and my afternoons working with the horses. I shifted my run to four in the afternoon when the temps were tolerable. That also allowed me to take in the sunset. Once in a while, Chase and I enjoyed a ride that included congenial conversation and sometimes teasing banter. My discomfort in his presence disappeared, but I couldn't pin down exactly when it had.

He never broached the subject of wanting to kiss me, but now and then I caught a glimmer of that desire in his eyes. Each time I did, my stomach flip-flopped. When I tried to imagine where our relationship might go, it was like having writer's block. My mind went blank.

So I sought God's guidance. The only words I sensed in my spirit were *embrace your inheritance*. What did that mean exactly? Accept, agree with, become a part of? Allow a romantic relationship to develop? I turned to the dictionary to gain a deeper grasp on the meaning of *embrace*. Then I searched for the word in the Bible and discovered it eight times in the King James, always in reference to the same Hebrew word that meant *to clasp*. To clasp something was to take hold of it.

God wanted me to take a hold of my inheritance. Grabbing hold of it indicated my acceptance of it as a part of my life. Not just the financial aspects, but Abby and Chase and his family as well. Creating the life I wanted started with using my power of choice. God said *embrace your inheritance*, but I first had to make the decision to do just that.

I didn't know how I felt about Chase, but I decided to keep the door open to a romantic relationship rather than erect a wall.

Having confronted and resolved these questions, I felt less and less like an ant invading the palace. Yet a sense of disaster ahead nagged at me. Where was that coming from? Was it merely self-sabotage or Holy Spirit warning me of difficulties ahead?

The Monday afternoon before Thanksgiving, Chase came to my room with a letter in his hand.

He held it up. "Let's go for ride. I have some news."

"News? What news would you get that you'd need to discuss with me?"

"Jake's trial."

"Oh," I said flatly. I hit ctrl+s on my keyboard to save my work then shut my laptop. Chase waited while I pulled on my cowboy boots, donned my Stetson, and grabbed my jacket from the bed post. Together we walked to the barn.

"I got a summons to Jake's trial," Chase said as we walked. "I'm sure you'll get one too, but it's probably been delayed in the forwarding process. I think it would be a good idea to let the attorneys involved know that you're here in Great Falls so they can direct any mail here instead of to Kansas City."

"Definitely. I'd forgotten all about the situation with Jake. I guess I figured there wouldn't be a trial because he admitted to trying to kill me."

"He admitted that to you out there on the range, but when he was taken in by the police, they took him directly for a psych evaluation. As far as I know, he never admitted anything to the police."

We gathered the necessary bridles and saddles from the tack room. Sandy whinnied and pranced around in her stall when I approached. "Hello, girl. I can see you're rarin' to go for a ride." I draped the bridle on a hook next to the stall gate, and then set the saddle on the floor.

"A person would think you've been doing this all your life." Chase winked at me from beside Molly's stall.

We bridled and saddled the horses in silence, pushing any further conversation to when we were on the open range. Obviously if there was going to be a trial, I'd have to testify. After all, it was me he had tried to kill.

We led the horses out of the barn, mounted, and nudged them into a slow walk.

"When's the trial?" I asked, finally breaking the heavy silence.

"February 20. I'm on the witness list, though don't know what I can contribute. I didn't directly witness anything. Now you? That's another story. You going to be okay with all this?"

"Of course. It's not the first time I've had to give testimony. At least it's after Emily's wedding and Christmas."

"Yes. I'll give Abby a call when we get back and let her know about this."

But he didn't have to call Abby because she was waiting at the barn when we galloped in laughing from another race.

"Abby, I was just going to call you." Chase dismounted. "Is everything all right? You look upset."

"I've just had a call from Leslie about Jake."

"Yeah, I got notice today of his trial date. How's Leslie doing?"

"Surprisingly well. But it isn't the trial date she called to tell me about. It has to do with Sally."

I jerked my head back. "Me? What about me?" I dismounted.

"Jake filed assault charges against you."

"Assault charges? That's ridiculous. I never assaulted him." How could a man who had attempted to murder me—twice no less—claim I had assaulted him? Even behind bars he was causing me trouble. How long would this go on?

"You know, for a man who's divorcing his wife, Jake sure keeps Leslie informed about a lot." Chase stood shaking his head.

"Meetings with the lawyer," Abby explained. "The same one handling the trial is handling the divorce."

"But when and how did I ever assault Jake?"

The three of us stood there thinking back over the events of August. Then it struck me. "I sprayed his face with bear spray. As far as I'm concerned, an act of self-defense since he had a revolver pointed at me."

"And since it was only the two of you when it happened, it's a case of he-said she-said." Chase looked around the yard. "Gabe," he hollered.

Gabe jogged out from the barn. "Yeah, Pop?"

"Take care of horses, please. Something's come up." Chase handed over Molly's reins. Gabe took them, then took Sandy's from me and led the horses into the barn. Chase, Abby, and I headed toward the house.

"Now it's even more important to let the court know where I can be found," I said. "I don't want to get arrested for missing an appearance."

"Wait a minute." Chase stopped and turned toward Abby. "You said *filed,* as in it's a done deal? Did Leslie say whether a hearing had been scheduled?"

"No, she didn't."

"Then we'd better find out who Jake's lawyer is and call him ASAP. Sally's right. It wouldn't be good for her to miss court, no matter what the excuse."

I marveled that Jake had been found competent to stand trial. Nothing he did made sense to me. Filing for divorce from Leslie, whom he considered his meal ticket. That was the reason he tried to kill me, so my share of the inheritance would revert to Leslie. Now he was filing charges against me for what was clearly an act of self-defense on my part. No doubt he hoped to gain large financial settlements in both instances, but how could he enjoy them while incarcerated? I guess he didn't expect to be found guilty of attempted murder. Yet another factor that caused me to question his sanity.

We made a beeline for Chase's office. By the time Abby found out the name of Jake's lawyer his office had closed for the day. I'd have to call first thing tomorrow morning because more than likely, the lawyer's office and the courthouse would be closed on Wednesday for Thanksgiving.

I assured myself this latest setback was no biggie, a fly in the ointment as I'd heard Chase say so often during the trail drive. I decided not to let it ruin the day or the upcoming holidays.

The following morning I called the lawyer's office promptly at 8:00.

"Good morning. Miller and Shane Law Offices. How may I help you?"

"Good morning. My name is Sally Clark. I understand Mr. Miller is handling a case for Jake Bonner on assault charges against me. I need to let him know my current address is here in Great Falls. I also need to find out what court the case was filed in so I can update them on my address as well."

"I can take your address, then you'll want to contact the Clerk of the District Court."

I gave her Chase's address, and she was kind enough to give me the number for the district court. After I spoke with the court clerk, I decided it was time to get a lawyer. Mark Brown came to mind, but he lived in Nebraska and more than likely wasn't licensed to practice law in Montana. Karl Kandell, Chase's lawyer, could probably recommend someone.

"Kandell Law Offices, how may I help you?"

"Good morning, this is Sally Clark."

"Good morning, Miss Clark. How are you?" She obviously remembered me from my visit to the Kandell Law Office in August.

"I'm fine but in need of a lawyer. Are you aware of the situation with Jake Bonner?"

"I know he was found competent for trial, and that it's set for February 20. But there's no need for you to have a lawyer for that."

"Oh, I know, but he's filed assault charges against me. I found out yesterday and just spoke to the court clerk. He told me the case is in the initial stages and that a summons hasn't yet been issued. Can Karl handle this or recommend someone who could?"

"Karl's case load is full, but we have a new man in the office who'd be perfect. Sounds like we'd better get you in today, if possible. Hold on while I pull up his calendar."

I waited momentarily while the receptionist checked for appointment times.

145

"He's had a cancellation. Can you be here at eleven?"

"Definitely. Thank you." I had an hour before I'd have to drive into town. I'd spend that time seeking the Lord's guidance.

I need Your help here, Papa.

Remember, My daughter, you can choose how you view this situation. You can see yourself as a victim or you can choose to be a creator, as I am. Instead of seeing this as good or bad, view this experience as a lesson.

A lesson? I heard my father say *I'll teach you a lesson!* many times when I was a child. You know that, and You know it was never a good thing. What have I done to rate Your punishment?

I am not punishing you. Your father used those words wrongly. A lesson is merely an experience that helps you learn something you need to know. And you choose whether the experience is good or bad or in-between. Recall what you told yourself yesterday: I won't let it ruin the holidays. The moment you chose the outcome you wanted, you became a creator of the life you want, instead of being a helpless victim.

Wow. Creator? Victim? Chase has mentioned those words before, but You haven't.

You weren't ready to hear them.

That challenged me. I couldn't remember God ever speaking to me on such a spiritual level as this. I liked it and meditated on those words until it was time for me to leave.

I let Chase know I had an appointment in town but didn't know what time I'd be back.

"Can you find your way around town okay?"

"It's time I learned."

My conversation with God had my adrenaline pumping. On the way into town, I quoted Psalm 91, something I'd done nearly every day when I was in the Middle East. He will deliver me from the snare of the fowler, and from the noisome pestilence.

Jake was certainly a noisome pestilence.

Only with my eyes will I look and see the reward of the wicked. ... No evil shall befall me. ...I will call upon the Lord and He will answer me; He will be with me in trouble; and He will deliver me and honor me.

No matter the outcome, I determined I would grow in positive ways through this experience. I walked into the lawyer's office with words from Shakespeare ringing in my ears. Once more unto the breach, dear friends.

"Good morning, Miss Clark. It's nice to meet you. I'm Roger McBride." He shook my hand. "Come on in and take a seat."

He took his seat behind his desk and leaned back in the mahogany leather chair. I took one of the two blue upholstered accent chairs in front of his desk.

"Cindy, tells me you've had an assault case filed against you. What details can you give me?" McBride's graying temple hairs indicated he was probably at least in his late forties, though he lacked the paunch typical of men that age. I hoped the gray at least indicated he was a man with several years' experience as a lawyer rather than fresh out of law school. That Karl had hired him said a lot. Karl was a tenacious lawyer.

"It's a civil case brought against me by Jake Bonner. His lawyer is Tim Miller. The only incident that comes remotely close to assault is when I sprayed Jake with bear spray."

"And why did you do that?"

"He had a gun pointed at me with the intent to kill."

McBride jerked forward in his chair. "He tried to kill you?"

"Yes. I'd taken a horseback ride out on Chase Reynold's ranch. Jake followed me. He was outfitted with a rifle and a revolver and admitted he planned to kill me. Spraying him with the bear spray is what allowed me to get away from him and back to safety at the ranch. Jake's currently awaiting trial for attempted murder against me."

"When is Mr. Bonner's criminal trial? Has a date been set?" McBride busily scribbled notes.

"February 20."

"Do you have an inkling on how strong a case the prosecution has?"

He started chewing on the tip of his pen.

"I'd say strong. Aside from my testimony, there's testimony from Four and Gabe Reynolds…and Toby, Jake's accomplice. Jake was initially evaluated to determine if he was competent to stand trial."

"Sounds cut and dried to me. The burden of proof for the assault charges lies with Mr. Bonner, or rather, his lawyer. Given the charges Mr. Bonner filed, I'd say it's safe to assume he plans to plead not guilty to attempted murder." McBride laid his pen down and leaned forward over his desk. "Why did he try to kill you?"

"Because of what I inherited from the Reynolds family. If I was dead, a portion of what I inherited would revert to Leslie, and the rest back to Chase and Abby."

"I'm new in town. Who are Leslie, Chase, and Abby?"

"I'm sorry. Leslie is currently Jake's wife, but he also recently filed for divorce."

"He's been a busy man." McBride jotted down the information.

"Chase Reynolds is Leslie's father, and Abby is her aunt."

"I trust the Reynolds family is worth big dollars? And Mr. Bonner wanted that for himself?"

"Yes. Multi-millions." I widened my eyes to make my point.

McBride leaned back in his chair and rocked a bit. "It's a good chance a judge will stay the civil case until after the criminal one. I'm surprised Mr. Bonner's lawyer didn't advise against filing the civil charges, but until I talk to him and find out exactly what assault he's claiming, we can't be sure of anything."

"*Stay* the civil case?"

"Sorry, legal jargon. Stop it from moving forward. Is the criminal case why you're here in town?"

"No, I'm simply here spending the holidays with the Reynolds family. I only just found out yesterday about Jake's trial because Chase got notice in the mail."

"Did the court fail to notify you?" He chewed on his pen again.

"I can't be sure of that. I live in Kansas City, so all my mail is being forwarded here. Probably just delayed in the process."

"Let me get your phone number and address; I'll be sure to notify the clerk."

"I already did" I gave him my number and address.

"Do you have any final questions?"

"When can I expect to hear anything about the status of Jake's claim?"

"The Thanksgiving holiday will slow things down, certainly. I'll connect with Mr. Miller as soon as we're done here. Have Cindy set an appointment for next week. If we don't need to meet, it's easier to cancel than find a place to fit you in."

I rose from my chair. "Thank you so much, Mr. McBride. I'm relieved to put this in your hands."

He stood and we shook hands. "Rest assured, Miss Clark, I don't think there's anything to worry about."

I drove home and set to work on my novel.

Later in the day, Mr. McBride called with the news that it was indeed the bear spray incident that Jake was claiming as assault. That increased the chances the judge would stay the case. I'd forgotten about the incidents of vandalism at the ranch that were also Jake's doing but that he'd accused me of, so quickly passed on those specifics.

A peace settled over me when I ended the call. Maybe it was God's assurance or simply the fact that I'd taken action for myself or both. It didn't matter. I felt good, more confident in myself and in the direction for my life.

Chapter Nineteen

SALLY

"Joyful are people of integrity, who follow the
instructions of the LORD." Psalm 119:1

Thanksgiving Day arrived and Chase's kids, their wives, and
the grandkids descended on the house. Easily enough for two
baseball teams. A large turkey to be roasted had garnered a
good deal of refrigerator space for several days prior. Michael brought
a second one he planned to deep fry. As much as I wanted to help, I
realized everyone had their tasks well in hand, and I would merely get
in the way.

The weather had turned cold with temps dipping into the twenties,
and a pewter gray sky hinted at snow. I corralled the kids near the
fireplace in the great room. They'd brought their favorite board games.
The eight-and-older kids set up Monopoly, and I enjoyed Chutes and
Ladders with those seven and under. The burning logs crackled and
popped and added a toasty warmth to the room. Before long the scent
of roasting turkey wafted into the room, eliciting "Mmm, that smells
good" and "I'm getting hungry" from several mouths.

Chase planned the big meal for one o' clock, and at noon, all games
came to a halt. Abby assigned a task to everyone, even little three-year-
old Heather who laid a cloth napkin at every plate. I watched it all
while I filled each glass with water. The smiles, the banter, the laughter
all spoke of the deep love, commitment, and bond this family had. My

heart ached that I hadn't known this as a child, yet delight overflowed that I shared in it now.

Like all the other meals, the two turkeys and all the side dishes were placed on the side board in the dining room. Extra tables had been set up to accommodate the overflow of people, the teenagers in the great room, and the littles in the dining room with the adults.

When it was time for dessert, I decided to make my big announcement. I rose from my chair. "Excuse me, everybody. I have an announcement." I waited for the chatter to end. "I wanted to let you all know I've decided to move here to Great Falls after New Year's. If anybody knows of a house for sale, let me know."

Cheers erupted.

"You can buy my house," Leslie said, bringing an abrupt end to the cheers.

"Why're you selling your house?" Four asked. "Do you need the money to pay Jake's legal fees?"

"No, but as you probably know, Jake has filed for divorce." Leslie hesitated and looked around the room at each frowning face.

"No, I didn't know," Four said. "How are you doing with that?"

"I filed a counter-petition. My lawyer also advised I wait to sell until after Jake's trial, and I will, but the house is in my name. She says I have a good chance of keeping Jake's financial claims in the divorce to a minimum, but I can't live there anymore. Too many reminders."

Words of commiseration traveled around the table.

"I'm fine, really I am. Jake filing for divorce forced me to look at our marriage. I didn't realize how miserable I'd become. I'll spare you the details, but it's all good. And, Sally, I'm sure you don't want my house, but I'll give you my Realtor's name if you like."

To say that offer surprised me would be an understatement. It left me momentarily speechless. Leslie had treated me with such disdain when I first arrived in August because she expected the share in *Cowboy & Cattle* magazine that I received. She knew if I didn't complete my qualifying four weeks at the ranch, my share reverted to her. And to that end, she did all she could to get me to leave early, including planting $1000 from the magazine's petty cash box in my purse to get me arrested for theft.

She had eventually come to her senses, confessed what she'd done, and apologized. Her behavior toward me had done an about-face I was still coming to terms with. "Thank you, Leslie. I'd like that."

Abby rose from her chair, gave Leslie a hug, then came and hugged me. "I'm so delighted you're moving here! What fun we're going to have."

"Fun? You say that like you've got something sneaky up your sleeve." I squinted at her.

Abby laughed. "I only meant shopping and girl talk. Decorating your new house. But maybe we can pull a prank or two on Chase." She winked and returned to her seat.

Several family members related their pleasure with my decision. Gabe and Pete hugged me like they'd found a long-lost teddy bear. My heart quivered and a warmth radiated throughout my body. Is this what being loved and accepted felt like?

Chapter Twenty

CHASE

"Never let loyalty and kindness leave you! Tie them around your neck as a reminder. Write them deep within your heart." Proverbs 3:3

My late wife, Karen, and I always enjoyed the excitement of the holidays. She'd be reveling in the activity that now filled the house. My heart ached that she wasn't here to enjoy it, that she never had the opportunity to meet the three newest grandkids. I watched with contentment and joy as the house filled with my children, their wives, and my grandchildren. We did good, Karen. I hope you're looking down on today with joy.

Activity buzzed everywhere, but especially in the kitchen. I learned many years ago to stay out of the way when the women were cooking, so I observed from the doorway. In recent years, my son Michael had joined the "chefs." He busily slathered spices onto his turkey, prepping it for deep-frying. My daughters-in-law, Hannah and Linda, stood next to each other chatting while one peeled potatoes and the other chopped salad ingredients.

Abby had arrived with three pumpkin pies along with the requisite whipped cream and now busied herself with preparing sage stuffing, though we never stuffed our turkey. My stomach growled thinking about all the delicious food I'd scoop onto my plate in a few short hours.

I heard laughter from the great room and meandered in to join the fun. Sally sat with the younger kids playing Chutes and Ladders. The rest were deep into a game of Monopoly.

"Is it too late for me to join the Monopoly game?" I didn't want to make Sally nervous by joining in with her.

"There's only one piece of property left to buy, Grampa. Are you good with that?" My oldest grandson looked up from his position on the floor.

"I think I can handle that." I grabbed a pillow from the couch, tossed it onto the floor, and got as comfortable as I could.

The importance of family was the legacy my father had passed to me, and I prayed I was passing to my children and grandchildren.

"Look, Grampa, look!" squealed three-year-old Heather. She stood at the window, bouncing with excitement. "It's snowing."

Everyone looked up from what they were doing and several rose and joined Heather at the window. I scooped her into my arms. "It sure is, Button. As hard as it's snowing, maybe there'll be enough snow to build a snowman after we eat."

"Can I skip my nap? …Pleeeeease."

"That's up to your mommy, but I'll see what I can do."

She kissed my cheek then hugged my neck.

"Come on, Grampa, it's your turn."

I gave Heather a gentle squeeze, set her down, and playfully ruffled her hair. I looked down at Sally who had maintained her position on the floor, though all her players had deserted her to watch the falling snow. A smile graced her face as she observed the little ones jumping around in excitement about the snow. What was she thinking? What had Thanksgiving been like at her home before her mother died? And after?

"Graaaampaaa, you're holding up our game."

"Okay, okay. I'm coming." I gave the impatient grandson a mild noogie before sitting back down.

"Grampa," he protested, then giggled.

I snatched the dice from the board, rolled, then landed firmly on Go to Jail.

"Go directly to jail. Do not pass go. Do not collect $200." The same impatient grandson laughed. "Are ya gonna pay to get out or take your chances on rolling doubles?"

But my thoughts had shifted to Jake, who currently *was* sitting in jail awaiting trial.

Fun and food filled Thanksgiving Day and Sally's announcement topped it all. Christmas promised even more food and excitement with Emily's wedding on Christmas Eve.

The Monday after Thanksgiving, I pulled my tux from the closet and sent it to the cleaners in preparation for the wedding. I'd be walking my youngest down the aisle. The last wedding I'd pay for but surely not the last I would attend. Peter and Gabe had yet to tie the knot with someone. If they were waiting for twin sisters, it might never happen. But then, nothing is impossible for God.

In the three weeks since Abby returned home, Emily's and Leslie's frantic calls to Gabe and Peter had ended. I came to the same conclusion the boys had: Abby had a calming presence in Emily's and Leslie's lives. But what toll did that take on her? I decided to give her a call.

"Hi, Chase."

"Hey, Abby. Not catching you at a bad time am I?"

"Not at all. What do you need?"

"I don't need anything. I called to see how you're doing. I just got back from dropping my tux at the dry cleaners, and I remembered Gabe saying Emily and Leslie driving him and Pete crazy with phone calls every day while you were gone. Are they driving you mad?"

Abby laughed. "A bit the first week I was back, but all's good now. Leslie's announcement during our Thanksgiving meal shocked me. Chase, this may sound odd, but she seems to have grown up."

"That's what's different! I couldn't quite put my finger on it, but you're right. You're a wonderful aunt, you know that, don't you?"

"Of course I do." Abby's smile infected her voice. "You've told me many times before, and so did Karen before she died."

157

"And you'll hear it plenty more before it's all done. Is Cohen coming for the wedding?"

"Yes, and his daughter, Hannah. Are you sure you're okay with them staying at the ranch and spending Christmas and New Year's with us? I've got room at my place, you know."

"It's fine. Better here for propriety's sake if anything. It'll give him a good taste of the Reynolds clan. Think he'll survive?"

"Only if you and Sally don't gang up on him."

"I promise. And I'll talk to Sally, tell her to temper that warrior spirit that seems to reside in her heart."

"I think God has softened that side of her in the past month...a lot."

"Yeah. Now that you mention it, I don't think I've heard a snarky comment from her since our dinner date in Scottsbluff."

I'd grown to love Sally's fighting spirit. She let nothing stop her from the goals she set for herself. What equated to a softened heart, I think, was that she had let down her guard to a large degree. Thankfully that warrior in her only very briefly went AWOL during our date.

Chapter Twenty-One

SALLY

"The eyes of the LORD watch over those who do right; his
ears are open to their cries for help." Psalm 34:15

The Monday after Thanksgiving, I called Leslie's Realtor from
the privacy of my bedroom. We talked about what I wanted in
a house and about getting pre-qualified for a loan.

"I'll be using the VA for my loan. I recently quit my job so I can
write full-time. Will that cause any problems?"

"It could. Your current financial health will have a bearing. Do you
have any money coming in?"

"I inherited quarterly payouts from *Cattle & Cowboy* and a yearly
payout from the Reynolds' ranch. Oh, and I have rental property in
Nebraska."

"How much is all that yearly?" she asked.

"I don't know. I received the inheritance from Mr. Reynolds in August and only one payout since then."

"Okay. If you can get some paperwork on what those payouts were
last year, that will help. Any other issues you think might get in the way?"

"I have assault charges pending against me. I suppose there's a minor possibility I might owe financial remunerations."

"Oh my goodness!"

The line went silent. Was the real estate agent wondering what kind
of woman I was to have been charged with assault? Did she think I'd be

a safety risk to her or was she evaluating whether I fit her ideal client profile?

"That could have a major impact on getting pre-qualified. And I'd hate to see you forced to sell the house right after you buy it."

"That's not going to happen. The charge has no merit. The man was trying to kill me."

"Oh, dear. Well...I..."

I had only made the situation worse.

"Why don't you give me a call once all that has been settled?"

"I can do that. Thank you for your time." I hung up. I'd probably get the same response from every other real estate agent I might call—unless I omitted telling them about the assault case. But omitting something is the same as lying.

Surely any judge would see through the foolishness of Jake's charge against me and deny it or throw it out or whatever the legal term was. I could hardly wait for Jake's trial for first-degree attempted murder to roll around and to hear the judge say guilty and sentence him to life in prison. That was the wrong attitude for me to have, but that's how I felt. I could forgive Jake, but that didn't mean the consequences of his actions would magically disappear. It only meant I wouldn't carry around any emotional baggage from the situation.

In the meantime, I'd conduct my own house search. Maybe I could scrounge enough money together to pay cash and not need a demanding bank's approval for a loan. I had $200K in the bank right now that I could slap down on a house. I wasn't going to let Jake's little stunt stop me.

Moments later Mark Brown called.

"Hi, Mark. What's up?"

"I heard back on the petition to open your brother's adoption records. Bad news I'm afraid."

"They denied it?"

"Yes. I'm sorry. I knew last week but didn't want to ruin your Thanksgiving."

"Thank you, I appreciate your concern. Any other ideas on how we might find him?"

"Not at the moment, but I'll keep thinking."

"Have you made any headway on finding out about my biological parents and the sale of their business?"

"Very little. Most of the records from back then have yet to be digitized, so it's a matter of searching through the archives in the courthouse basement. Between my other cases, I'm sorry I just haven't had much time."

"Okay, no worries. Have a nice week. Goodbye." I clicked off the call. At least I had the picture of the three of us at the orphanage, but today it seemed like the odds were against me. My emotional storm had subsided a couple weeks ago, but today it raged back.

Had God closed this door or had the devil? Maybe my orphan brother Robert wasn't a good person. Maybe he'd only bring trouble into my life. But the opposite of that was just as likely.

I dropped back in the chair, frustrated. I reviewed the events of the year. My New Year's resolution had been to seek the abundant life Jesus died to give me. It looked ready to arrive when Mr. Pendrake said he planned to promote me to editorial director of Pendrake Publishing. But then he died in March and all his plans for the company died with him. The new CEO micromanaged and made a job I once enjoyed into one of misery.

Then came the inheritance—that nearly cost me my life—my father's death, being stranded by a blizzard for three and a half days, and now Jake's lawsuit against me.

Wait a minute! Was this victim thinking? Probably. There had to be a positive side to each of these.

I dialed Abby. I needed to let her know about the petition, but I also knew she could advise me on how to focus my thoughts.

"Hi, Sally. How are you?"

"I'm okay. I just heard from Mark about Robert's adoption records. The petition was denied."

"Oh…how disappointing. Now what do we do? Are you committed to finding him no matter the obstacles you run into?"

"That's a loaded question. I think I am, but I'm struggling this morning. Maybe God closed that door for a reason. Maybe Robert is some kind of crook or a mean and abusive man."

"And I'm going to go back to my question. Are you still committed, deep down, to finding Robert no matter what?"

Was I? I took a deep breath and rubbed the back of my neck. Was finding Robert as important to Abby as it was to me? "Yes, I am. Are you? And be honest."

"Yes."

"Abby, how hard has it been for you to come to grips with finding out so late in life that you were adopted? I'm sorry I haven't asked before now. Surely, you've struggled with some of this."

Abby was silent, but I could hear background noise from the office.

"I'm sorry, I shouldn't have interrupted your day. We can talk about this some other time. But I wanted you to know about the petition."

"No, it's fine. I'm preoccupied thinking about Cohen. He and Hannah will be coming for the wedding and will stay through New Year's."

"Wow. It'll be full house at the ranch. Or will they stay with you?"

"The ranch, but he insisted on driving. Pray for good weather."

I laughed. "Yeah, I think we've had our fill of snow for this season."

"Christmas won't get here fast enough for me. I'm tired of FaceTiming." Abby's deflated tone made me wonder if she was lovesick, and I wondered how far their relationship had progressed in the six weeks since meeting him. If I'd been in the room with her, I might have spotted a melancholy look in her eyes. But now I felt uncomfortable about asking her how I could get out of my own emotional funk.

"Christmas is only four weeks away. In the meantime, why don't we do a DNA test? That might connect us with Robert if he's done one, too, and it might point us to other family members as well."

"It's a thought. Do some research and then let's talk more."

"Okay. I'll let you get back to work. Talk to you later." I hung up, wishing I could cheer her up. How had their relationship progressed so far so quickly? I remembered the look that passed between them the day of the blizzard when they first set eyes on each other. That exchange carried enough energy to compete with a bolt of lightning. That man had better not break her heart.

I needed some distraction therapy. I turned my energy toward researching DNA testing. Who might I discover in the process?

DNA research turned out to be more complicated than I realized. I found an online guide and moved forward with researching companies. I also realized they'd need only my DNA. I let Abby know I was moving forward. I sent off for the test, did what it required the day it arrived in the mail, and sent it back. Now to wait for the results.

In the days to Christmas, I did more research on my biological parents, the Leonards, and found a couple of pictures of George Leonard at his feedstore. In each picture, he wore a gray bucket hat, a few fishing flies decorating it. The hat looked familiar, but I couldn't put my finger on why. The fishing flies indicated he liked to fish. Maybe I had inherited my love of nature from him.

Abby had her hands full with running the magazine and keeping Emily and Leslie on an even emotional keel. How did she do it? I offered to help, but in the end there was little I could do. I prayed Cohen provided her with what support he could from a distance.

For me, the days to Christmas passed quickly. During my quiet times, I looked for the positives of the year and knew that the most positive thing had been discovering my twin sister, and I had the finances that would allow me to write full time.

I continued working on my novel in the mornings and with the horses in the afternoons. I also spent some time researching homes for sale. Chase and I actually viewed several together. He gave his advice about the best parts of town and those to avoid. The city's crime rate shocked me, but then it wasn't much different from Kansas City.

I got notice that the judge stayed Jake's assault charges. Mr. McBride had expected as much. To me, that pointed to the prosecutor having a strong case of convicting Jake of attempted murder. Maybe that was a wrong assumption on my part, but that and the fact that the judge refused Jake bail brought me some peace. I breathed a sigh of relief. I didn't like the idea of him roaming Great Falls to commit whatever other offense against me he might fancy.

Neither Abby nor I had heard anything from Elizabeth Travers. Not even a notice as to when her interview with Abby and Cohen would air. All the potential pitfalls that might impact the joy of the season fell to the wayside. Thank you, Jesus!

Ten days before Christmas, I turned my attention to what gifts to buy Chase and his kids. That took some brain-wracking, I can tell you. They had everything they needed, and wanted for nothing. I plied Rita for her suggestions.

"I think you being here is gift enough for them."

"That's sweet of you to say, Rita. But surely there's something I can get them."

"What could you give that would be totally you?"

I thought for a moment. "There's a cookie my mom used to bake only at Christmas time. After she died, my friend and her mom helped me keep that tradition."

"I usually make sugar cookies at Christmas. What did you make?"

"Spritz cookies flavored with anise."

"Then do it. The guys rarely come into the kitchen, but I'll do what I can to help you get it done in secret. Maybe you could bake them at Abby's."

"Rita, that's a great idea! When does the tree go up? Do you put up a real one or fake?"

"Often it's a fake one. I'm surprised Chase hasn't already dug everything out of the basement. He usually has the tree up by now."

"Let me buy a real one. I haven't done a real tree in over a decade. It's time." And so it was decided. I informed Chase to save him the trouble of pulling the fake one out of storage with the other Christmas items.

I hadn't baked spritz in years, and with Chase's large family, I'd have to make three or four batches. An all-day endeavor to be sure. I looked up a recipe online and drove into town to buy the ingredients and gift boxes along with the tree. I returned having purchased a beautiful ten foot Douglas fir, entirely too large to tie to the roof of my car. A delivery driver pulled into the drive two minutes behind me.

I usually spent Christmas with my friends Jen and John unless they went out of town to their parents' houses. Suddenly Christmas took on a whole new level of excitement.

Chapter Twenty-Two
CHASE

"Who can find a virtuous and capable wife? She is
more precious than rubies." Proverbs 31:10

After my conversation with Abby about going easy on Cohen,
I went looking for Sally. I found her in her room, door open,
tapping away at her laptop.

"Knock, knock."

She looked up from her work. "Hi, Chase. What's up?"

"Nothing much." I leaned against the door frame. "Just talked with
Abby. It's a definite that Cohen and Hannah will be coming for the
wedding."

"Yeah, I know. Abby and I talked earlier this morning. She is beyond ready to see Cohen."

I jerked up from the door frame. "What do you mean by that?"

"She said she was tired of FaceTiming. Honestly, she sounded lovesick to me."

"May I?" I pointed to the foot of the bed. Sally occupied the only
chair in the room.

"Sure." She sat back in the chair and took a drink of coffee from the
cup on the end table. Was it even still warm?

I took a seat. "I thought she was only teasing when she asked that
you and I not gang up on him, but that puts a new spin on things."

"What do you mean 'not gang up on him'?"

"I teased her about whether Cohen could survive the Reynolds clan. You saw how full the house was on Thanksgiving. Her response was 'only if you and Sally don't gang up on him.' I promised we wouldn't."

"Okay, I promise. But he'd better not call me crazy again." She chuckled. "Which he hasn't since our last day at the church."

"Bite your tongue if you have to."

"Ouch. I'll do my best."

"How's your writing coming along?"

"Good. Up to 20,000 words already."

"Wow, I struggle to write an email. What's it about?"

She smiled and peered into the hallway as if determining if anyone was eavesdropping. "Don't tell Pete and Gabe, but I'm writing a romance about twin brothers who want to find twin sisters to marry."

I let out a laugh. "I'm glad my comment about them inspired you."

I laughed some more, rose from the bed, and left her to her writing.

As the days to Christmas passed, Sally grew more excited. Her excitement rivaled that of the grandkids. Her eyes sparkled and a smile had taken permanent residence on her lips. I often caught her humming a Christmas song. She had enjoyed Thanksgiving so maybe she was just looking forward to more of the same on Christmas. Maybe the words she needed for her book flowed like fire from her fingers. I saw her typing faster than I'd ever seen Abby type, and she could type.

What had Christmas been like for Sally? Knowing she hadn't returned home at all during her time in the Marines, what had Christmas been like then? Did she spend it alone on the base with Christmas dinner at the base dining hall? How did she spend the holiday after she got out of the Marines?

Maybe enthusiasm about the picture she had to give to Abby animated her behavior. She told me at supper one evening that her petition for her brother's adoption records had been denied, but also that she had decided to do a DNA test as a next step to finding him. Regardless of this drawback, she seemed positive about finding him.

It's all about family, Holy Spirit whispered to my soul.

Of course! Sally had embraced us as family, and that lay at the heart of her enthusiasm. Was she cognizant of that?

Like everyone else, I filled my spare time with shopping for gifts. The moment Sally announced she was moving to Great Falls, I decided what I'd give her. But it couldn't be wrapped or put under the tree. How could I deliver it in a unique way that would communicate how special she was to me?

One morning when she told me she was off to buy a Christmas tree, it dawned on me that preparations for Emily's wedding had overshadowed the holiday. I hadn't done any of my usual preparations. Karen had been in charge of decorations, but the tree was my responsibility. Since her death, I'd taken it all on. While Sally was in town tree shopping, I dug all the decorations out of the basement and carried them to the great room where the bulk of our festivities would take place.

When she pulled up to the front door with a delivery pickup truck behind her, her excitement erupted like a new oil well. Her eyes danced. She chattered like a chipmunk about decorating the tree and helping Rita bake Christmas goodies. Had she had a Grinch moment, her heart growing three sizes bigger?

Her glee infected me, and we laughed as we wrangled the tree to the great room. Its scent quickly permeated the room. Sally started Christmas music on her phone, which set the mood perfectly. Together we decorated the tree and decked out the room.

"Hey, you two, how about some peppermint hot chocolate?" Rita held out a tray with two mugs of steaming cocoa. "You've been at this for three hours. Looks magnificent, by the way."

Fake holly and white Christmas lights festooned the mantle, and I hung the six stockings Karen had made each of our kids. Christmas caroler and Santa Claus candles decorated the end tables. Red garland rounded the tree, along with white lights. Sally had placed red, blue, and green ornaments and then thrown tinsel onto its boughs as if she were planting wildflowers.

"Peppermint hot chocolate? Sounds scrumptious." Sally took a mug.

I grabbed a mug and turned to admire our handiwork, then took a seat to catch my breath. "We're not quite done. When's lunch, Rita?"

"I served lunch an hour ago. Gabe said he didn't want to interrupt your fun. I haven't cleaned up yet, and there's plenty left."

"Let's grab a quick bite, Sally, and finish this afterwards."

"But I'm helping Rita decorate her sugar cookies this afternoon."

"Those cookies won't be goin' anywhere, hon. You can help after you're done in here," Rita said.

"You're sure?"

"I'm sure," Rita said to Sally though her eyes met mine. She tipped her head slightly as if to say you two belong together. She turned and headed back to the kitchen.

I rose from the chair, wrapped my arm around Sally's waist, and led her to the dining room.

A new normal settled in my gut that morning. I'd been seeking one since the day Pop died five months ago and Sally entered our lives. I drew a deep breath and savored the moment.

Would I have to find another new normal when Sally moved into her own house somewhere else in Great Falls?

Cohen and his daughter arrived two days before Emily's wedding. I showed them to their respective bedrooms. I left Cohen to unpack his suitcases and took Hannah to the barn to meet the horses…and Gabe and Pete. She took to the horses instantly. I returned to the house alone.

Rita had been busy all week baking melt-in-your-mouth sugar cookies—and Sally decorated each one—Christmas stollen, and heaps of cinnamon rolls for Christmas morning breakfast that we'd eat while opening gifts. My stomach was in a constant state of hunger.

Finally, Emily's wedding day arrived. Abby, God bless her, had stepped in to do the things my wife would have had she been alive.

Abby often told me she considered my children as hers, and over the years she more than proved that. As I lay in bed that morning, I knew she and Emily were already up and busy with whatever preparations women do for a wedding.

At noon, Gabe, Pete, Sally, and I piled into my SUV truck to head for the church. The wedding was to start at one o' clock. The church teemed with guests. We never saw this many people at Sunday service. One of the ushers stepped up to escort Sally to the front pew, and Gabe and Pete followed them. I made my way downstairs to where I knew Emily would be making last minute preparations. I knocked on the door of the Sunday school room.

"Who is it?"

"Just me, pumpkin. Wanted to let you know I'm here."

The door opened and Abby appeared. Behind her stood Emily. My heart swelled and my eyes teared as I took in the beautiful young woman who stood before me. I stepped into the room.

"You look absolutely stunning, sweetheart." I gently kissed her cheek. "I wish your mother was here to see you."

"Oh, Pop, please don't make me cry. I wish she was too."

"She's looking down on us all from heaven," Abby said. "Now out, Chase, before we're all in tears."

I made haste to the door before Abby took a broom to me.

Ten minutes later, the bridesmaids, Abby, and Emily entered the church lobby. I watched as Abby fluffed one spot then smoothed another on Emily's wedding dress in final preparation for her walk down the aisle to her husband-to-be. Emily's face glowed with a joy and serenity that only come with the assurance of being in God's perfect will.

The glow on Abby's face rivaled Emily's. The reason for that sat next to Sally in the front pew.

Meanwhile, I wondered if my face was turning blue. I tugged at the tuxedo bow tie strangling me, hoping to find some breathing room. If I didn't find tying it so darned convoluted, I would have untied it and started again, but I'd run out of time.

"Are you ready, pumpkin?" I didn't need to ask, but I did anyway.

"You know I am, Pop. But you look as nervous as a calf facing a branding iron. What's with that?"

"Being in a tuxedo *is* like being branded. Let's get this started."

The organist expertly keyed a song I recognized as classical music. The bridesmaids walked the aisle and took their places.

I tucked Emily's arm in the crook of my elbow and we presented ourselves at the sanctuary entrance. The pastor gave a slight nod to the church organist and the first note of the "Wedding March" boomed through the church, leaving my insides vibrating.

As we promenaded down the aisle, I observed the crowd. Three hundred invites had gone out and I think all had opted to attend, plus some. The sanctuary was as full as the river during spring thaw. Smiles greeted us.

Matt, Emily's husband-to-be, also looked like a calf at branding time. His clenched jaw relaxed the moment I handed Emily to him and took my seat on the pew next to Sally, Abby, and Cohen. As the ceremony began, the color returned to his face.

The wedding went off without a hitch—except the getting hitched that was supposed to happen. Now the attendees packed the reception hall. My arm felt numb from all the hands I shook as guests worked their way through the receiving line. I flexed my hand to get the blood flowing and stepped into the hall. Guests filled the tables and others milled around the room.

I took my seat at the appointed table, glad to be off my feet. I leaned toward Abby sitting next to me. "Where's Sally?"

"I don't know. She went off to the restroom while I was in the receiving line, and I haven't seen her since."

"Did I forget to tell her she was to sit with us?" I searched the room for her. I spotted Peter and Gabe, each with a date on their arm; Michael and Four with their wives; and the myriad of friends Emily and Matt had invited to witness their vows.

"I don't think so. At any rate, I reminded her as we left the church."

"Could she be sick?"

"No. I'm sure she's fine. Relax."

The clinking of a glass cut off any further conversation and the best man rose to give his toast. The festivities proceeded, all the appropriate toasts were made, including my very short speech, and then the DJ announced the couple's first dance.

I turned my attention to Emily, a mini version of her mother. How my wife would have enjoyed watching her daughter walk down that aisle on my arm. At least she had enjoyed that privilege with Leslie's wedding. As Matt twirled Emily around the dance floor, their faces exuded the love and passion they had for one another. A smile had not been absent from Emily's lips all afternoon. When their dance ended, the crowd broke into applause. The music continued and the wedding party rose and joined them on the floor.

I scanned the room again for Sally. Chairs lined the walls, but she had managed to find a bare spot and plastered herself against the wall near the doorway. Did she plan to make a quick escape? I followed her line of sight to the now full dance floor.

Sally might have considered herself a wallflower, but far from it. She wore that same stunning blue dress she'd worn the night I took her to dinner in Scottsbluff. I couldn't keep my eyes off her, then or now. Never in a million miles on the trail did I expect to fall in love with her.

I remembered how much I struggled during her initial four weeks at the ranch. I'd only recently learned Abby was adopted, so falling for Sally was like being in love with my sister. Not good. Identical twins with the same temperament, but with very different personalities. That posed its own problems because I constantly expected Sally to act like Abby. As chaotic as Sally's emotions had been in recent months, mine had been nearly so in August. Dealing with Pop's sudden death, then the revelation of Abby's adoption, and—the cherry on top—that she had a twin sister took its toll.

At the end of those four weeks I'd suspected I was falling in love, but now, I knew.

I rose and made my way over to her. "Sally, you look like a rabbit cornered by a fox. Has something upset you?"

"Goodness, do I really?" She put her hands to her cheeks. "I'm fine, but I feel very out of place. I barely know anyone here."

"There are a lot I don't know either, mostly Matt's friends and family I expect." At the risk of making her more nervous, I held out my hand to her. "May I have this dance?"

"Yes, you may." She smiled, took my hand, and we walked to a tiny empty spot on the dance floor.

We took our positions, and I stepped forward with Sally smoothly following my lead.

"It was a lovely ceremony. Matt seems like a perfect fit for Emily."

"Yes, he's solid. Abby's been quite impressed with his work at the magazine." I carefully maneuvered my way around the crowded floor, enjoying the feel of Sally in my arms.

"What are their honeymoon plans?"

"Last I knew, they plan to leave tomorrow afternoon for San Francisco after our Christmas Day celebrations."

"That sounds—" Sally's eyes locked on mine, her cheeks flushed, and she fell silent.

"A quarter for your thoughts." I smiled down at her.

She chuckled but didn't break eye contact. "Have you got one tucked in the pocket of that gorgeous tux you're wearing?"

"Sure do. Not gonna dig it out though. My hands are otherwise occupied."

"Yes, quite." Those Montana-sky-blue eyes of hers sparkled in the DJ's light flashing around the room. "I was thinking about my favorite Christmas movie, *White Christmas*, and the song Danny Kaye sings toward the beginning. 'The Best Things Happen While You're Dancing.'" She sang the title.

"Do they?" I whispered, wishing I could whirl her around like Danny Kaye had done with his dance partner. Too many people crowded the floor. Instead, I pulled her closer.

"They do," she whispered back.

I had to do something to distract myself from kissing her. I took the risk and twirled us through some fancy steps I remembered from my dancing days with my wife. Sally followed effortlessly. She appeared receptive to my desire to kiss her and might even have considered it romantic…if we'd been the only ones on the floor. But we were surrounded by hundreds of people and the accompanying cacophony. I wanted and needed a more solitary venue when I ventured our first kiss.

Chapter Twenty-Three
SALLY

"Take delight in the LORD, and he will give
you your heart's desires." Psalm 37:4

The warmth of Chase's arm at my waist sent a tingle through my stomach. Following his lead on the dance floor came like second nature. I'd done my share of dancing at Marine Corps Balls over the years but never the steps he took me through.

I hated that the only words crossing my lips were small talk. And what was I thinking with "The Best Things Happen While You're Dancing"! Never a rock to crawl under when I needed one.

But yearning filled his eyes. Then he sensually whispered, "Do they?"

When the words *they do* escaped my mouth, I wondered where they came from. How far down this road was I going to go?

His lips parted. Our clasped hands grew moist. I thought he was about to kiss me when, instead, he whirled me around the dance floor like Danny Kaye had Vera-Ellen in the movie. Twice now Chase had shown a desire to kiss me but didn't. Why?

However much I might have ached for that kiss, I would not initiate it. The physical tension between us increased by the second. Would the song ever end?

As the last note finally sounded, I plucked myself out of his arms, thinking it would break the tension, but it didn't. He frowned and his eyebrows creased.

"Is something wrong?"

"No," I blurted. "I...thanks. You're quite the dancer. Don't you have a dance with Emily?"

Another song started and the couple behind me bumped into me as they danced.

"Sorry," the guy said.

I moved off the floor. Chase followed.

My heart pounded. My body grew warm. My face was probably flushed and if anybody asked, I'd blame it on a hot flash, though I knew better. In all my years, I'd never experienced such a strong physical reaction to a man. It flustered me and I stood frozen in place, unsure my legs could carry me to the closest chair. I stared down at the floor.

"Sally, are you sure you're okay? You look like you're going to faint." Chase put his arm across my back.

I stiffened, but he didn't remove his arm. "I'm a bit overheated. I'm going outside for some fresh air."

"Okay, but if you're not back in ten minutes, I'm coming out to check on you."

I nodded my acknowledgment, glanced at my watch, and made my way outside. I paced the sidewalk, careful to avoid the crowds of people doing last-minute Christmas shopping. I stopped and took several long deep breaths and let my "hot flash" dissipate.

Sally, you've gone and fallen in love. What are you going to do now?

Christmas Eve night. I glanced at the clock on the bedside table. Make that Christmas morning. I lay in bed rehashing my fiasco at the wedding reception instead of thinking about the fun of Christmas day activities yet ahead.

Chase took my refusal to any further dancing in stride. He couldn't possibly have missed the emotion behind my physical discomfort. Our bodies had melded together as one when we danced, like we were always meant to be. Yet his nonchalance toward me afterward defied the desire that emanated from his eyes while we danced.

Was I misreading his body language?

My thoughts whirled. Fear gripped my stomach. There'd be no sleep tonight.

Protect yourself flashed through my mind. My stomach tightened. I recognized the voice as my own gut instinct advising me. I'd been protecting myself since Mom died.

While stranded by the blizzard, God had revealed and then decimated the foundation of anger I'd used all my life to survive. That anger provided a wall of protection. Now, with that wall gone, I recognized the foundation of fear that had fueled the anger. Fear of being rejected. Of being unlovable.

Sally, Chase was so right when he said you were alone because you wouldn't let anyone in, I chided myself.

All these years I had unconsciously kept people out of my life because if I didn't let them in, then they couldn't turn around later and reject me like my father had. If I didn't give Chase any opportunity to say I love you, then he couldn't later say I don't love you anymore. This belief was the "bullet" from my nightmare.

With that realization, my wall of protection collapsed like the walls of Jericho. A receptiveness permeated me, like fresh air rushing into a stale, dark, brick basement when a door is opened.

I had to focus on what I wanted out of life, not what I didn't want. On Thanksgiving Day, I glimpsed being loved and accepted and I wanted more of that.

"The truth is I am lovable. Jesus loved me so much He died for me," I whispered to myself.

I repeated those words again and again, and then a new thought came to me. I didn't even love myself, so how could I expect others to love me. Tears dribbled from the corners of my eyes and down my temples. "Papa, how do I learn to love myself?"

You are fearfully and wonderfully made. It is the warrior spirit within you that gives you that rough exterior you think is so unlovable. Embrace who I made you to be.

I told myself *I am fearfully and wonderfully made* until God's peace settled over me. I took a deep breath and rolled to my right side. Despite the calm that had settled in my mind, sleep seemed as far away as the moon.

I hadn't yet placed Abby's gift by the tree. Now was as good a time as any. Who knows, I might meet the jolly man himself in action. More likely, I'd meet Chase. Now that I was ready to let him in, so to speak, would he sense that difference?

The clock read 2:13. Chase had probably placed any last-minute gifts under the tree before going to bed. I'd run the risk.

I slipped on my robe and retrieved the wrapped poster from the closet. I tapped on my phone flashlight and tipped-toed downstairs to the great room. The tree lights had been left on and I stood to admire its beauty for several minutes. All white lights on a ten-foot tree, their brightness reflecting off red, green, and blue ornaments and twinkling off the tinsel that gently undulated in room's air.

A large star with a white light in the center and one at each of its five points topped the tree. The star that led the wise men to Christ, the light of the world. The beauty that was Christ's birth. His presence in the world. His death on the cross that brought me redemption, forgiveness, salvation, and so much more.

"Thank You, Jesus," I whispered.

You're welcome.

The instantaneousness of the response surprised me and a sense of love welled within me. I closed my eyes and relished it and the warmth and contentment it brought me.

"Sally, what are you doing?"

Chase's voice startled me and I nearly dropped Abby's gift. I aimed my flashlight at him. He stood at the far end of the room from where I was. "I couldn't sleep so decided I'd bring Abby's present down instead of waiting until later. What are *you* doing?"

"I couldn't sleep either. Came down for a glass of warm milk." He proffered said milk. "Do you need some help?"

"Not really. Just need to find a hole to set it in." I directed my flashlight from one side of the tree to the other. Presents galore wrapped in brightly colored paper and tied with ribbons, overflowed from beneath the tree. Several nestled within its green boughs.

Chase turned on a nearby lamp. "That should help."

"Yes, it does, thank you. Sorry I disturbed you."

"You didn't, but I saw the light moving around in the room and thought it might be a burglar."

"Burglars usually take things, not leave them." I hoped my attempt at a joke would lighten the tension in the room.

"Yes, so they do." He chuckled. "Good night." He turned to the hall-way and left the room.

Papa, don't let this tension between me and Chase ruin tomor-row...I mean this morning.

Chapter Twenty-Four

CHASE

"Joyful is the person who finds wisdom, the one
who gains understanding." Proverbs 3:13

Christmas morning started much like Thanksgiving Day except for the cinnamon rolls Rita had prepared for breakfast. I took a deep whiff of the cinnamon that wafted through the air as I made my way downstairs. Rita was at home with her own family so who had heated the rolls?

I unlocked the front door in preparation for the kids' arrival, then got the fire started in the great room. With that done, I ambled to the dining room. Gabe sat at the table, sipping a cup of coffee. "Morning, son. Thanks for heating some rolls."

"Morning, Pop." He yawned. "That was some wedding yesterday."

"It was." I squeezed his shoulder. "You gonna cross that threshold one day soon?"

He turned his head and gaped up at me. "Gotta have a girlfriend first."

I chuckled and helped myself to a roll and coffee. "That helps."

"You and Sally make a handsome couple. I watched you dance. You made some fancy moves for an old man."

"Hey, watch it. I'm not old."

He laughed. "If you say so. I didn't know you had it in you to dance like that."

"I'm full of surprises, son. I used to take your mother dancing all the time."

His eyes took on a far-off look.

"Something bothering you, Gabe?"

His eyes came back into focus. "Not really. Just seems love is in the air. You could barely put a fist between Aunt Abby and Cohen yesterday. And you and Sally are looking pretty sweet on each other too. I want to get married and have kids some day, but then I look at Leslie and Jake and I wonder if marriage is a road I want to travel."

"There's a reason wedding vows include the words 'for better or worse, in sickness and in health.' Marriage takes work *and commitment* from *both* partners. I don't think Jake ever had that kind of commitment to Leslie."

"Yeah, I think you're right. But all the same, I'm sure Leslie's heart is breaking right now."

"It is. How 'bout you do what you can to help her through it?"

"Sure thing, Pop. Did all that wisdom come with your age?" He grinned.

"Nope. Life experience and a lot of time in the Lord's Good Book."

The doorbell rang signaling the arrival of the kids and grandkids. They didn't wait for me to answer.

"Merry Christmas, Grandpa!" they hollered as they burst through the door. I hurried to the foyer. They'd already opened presents at home, but were just as excited about what was under the tree here. I smiled inwardly, enjoying their excitement but also my own.

I had a very special surprise for Sally. Yesterday afternoon, I had distinctly sensed her desire to kiss me as we danced, but then she shut me out. Another habitual act of protecting her heart? Would she receive my gift with the love I intended or refuse it? I'd better make hers the last gift opened so the grandkids would be occupied with their own gifts by then and be oblivious to all else.

The house quickly filled. Pete and Gabe carried in needed extra chairs from the dining room, and the grandkids plopped onto the floor, the littlest ones squealing their delight. Abby and Leslie carried in trays of cinnamon rolls, hot chocolate, and coffee.

Those who wanted breakfast grabbed a roll and a drink. When the little ones were done eating and had returned from washing their hands, I rose from my seat.

"All right, now that everyone has finished their breakfast, let the festivities begin." I rubbed my hands. "Who's going to play Santa Claus this year?"

Chapter Twenty-Five
SALLY

"Come, let us tell of the LORD's greatness; let us
exalt his name together." Psalm34:3

The shouts of eager children woke me around nine Christmas
morning. I had managed about six hours of sleep. I zipped to
the bathroom, washed my face, brushed my teeth, got dressed,
and went downstairs.

The great room bustled with people. Cohen and Hannah sat as
deeply scrunched into the couch as would allow. Cohen's tensed body
relaxed the moment he clapped eyes on me. I scanned the room for
Abby. I spotted the newlyweds—looking blissfully oblivious of everyone accept each other—ensconced in the loveseat on the wall opposite
the tree, but didn't see Abby anywhere.

"Is Abby not here yet?" I took a seat next to Hannah.

"She's in the kitchen preparing a tray of cinnamon rolls and drinks."
Cohen's knee bounced. "I never realized the family was this big."

"Relax." I clamped down on his knee to stop its bouncing. "They
won't bite. I feel a little awkward myself right now. But it'll be fine."

Abby entered the room bearing a large tray of mugs, steam rising
from each one. Leslie was right behind her with a tray loaded with
cinnamon rolls. Scents of pine, peppermint, and cinnamon battled
with each other to dominate the room. We all helped ourselves and
resumed our seats.

Once the little ones were done eating and had washed their hands, Chase rose from his chair.

"All right, now that everyone has finished their breakfast, let the festivities begin!" Chase rubbed his hands. "Who's going to play Santa Claus this year?"

Hands shot into the air, accompanied by shouts of "Me! Me!" from the children.

Chase looked at the raised hands, waving his index finger at each one. "Luke. You're on."

"Yes!" Luke fist-pumped then jumped up from the floor. I guessed him to be about ten or so. He strode to the tree, picked a gift, read the tag, then took it to the recipient. He handed out six gifts before anyone started ripping into the paper.

And so the morning progressed, punctuated by peals of laughter, gleeful squeals, and resounding thank yous.

I held my breath as Four opened my gift to him and his family. "Oooo, cookies." He held the box to his nose and took a long sniff. "Smells faintly of licorice. What kind of cookies are these?"

"Spritz, and they're flavored with anise. It's similar to licorice." I'd made six boxes, one for each of Chase's kids. Some held more to accommodate their family. I'd also made a box for Chase. "Everyone got the same thing from me. I didn't really know what you'd like, and Rita suggested something unique to me..."

Four popped one into his mouth and offered the box to his kids sitting nearby.

"They're shaped liked snowmen and Christmas trees. Sweet," one of the kids said.

"These are delicious." Four turned to his wife. "Get the recipe."

Gabe snatched a cookie from the box and tossed it into his mouth. "Mmmm. Luke, find my box."

So my cookies were a hit.

Lunchtime drew near before Luke got to the last gift: my poster picture to Abby. "This is kinda heavy." Luke struggled to lift it away from the wall I'd propped it against.

"Let me help." I jumped up from my seat. "It's my gift to Abby." Together we carried it over and set it on the floor in front of her.

"I don't get any cookies?" She sent me baleful puppy-dog eyes.

"I can make you some cookies," I consoled her, "but I think you'll like this much better. And it won't add to the waistline." I held it upright as she ripped off the wrapping and exposed the picture.

"I don't understand, Sally. Who are these people?" Abby said.

I noticed Cohen scoot forward on the couch and lean toward the photo for a better look. "What are you doing with a picture of Mark?"

"Don't be ridiculous. This isn't your brother-in-law. It's me, Abby, and our brother." I scowled at him.

Cohen pushed himself back off the edge of the couch. "Fooled me. I've seen a lot of his childhood pictures and that little kid is a dead ringer for Mark."

Abby stood, pulled the picture free of the remaining wrapping paper, and examined it. "Where did you get this?"

"The picture was in the box of stuff from my adoptive mom. I had it enlarged."

The room grew silent. I looked around, uncomfortable that all eyes were glued on us. Even the youngest kids perceived something transpiring that required their attention.

Abby's eyes widened. Her mouth dropped open and a quiet gasp escaped.

"I'm sorry you don't like it." How did I get it so wrong? I thought she'd be thrilled with the picture the same way I had been.

"Not like it? Oh, Sally, I love it." She handed the picture to Cohen and wrapped her arms around my neck. When she let go, I noticed a single tear trickle down her cheek. She smiled wanly, wiped the tear away, then took the picture from Cohen and turned it for everyone to see.

"Is that your mother holding you two?" Four's wife, Linda, asked.

"No, it's Mrs. Lowenfeld," I explained to the group. "The woman who ran the orphanage we were at. My adoptive mom wanted to adopt all three of us; her husband said no, only one. She grew up with Mrs. Lowenfeld and convinced her to take this picture for her to keep."

"How wonderful for her to leave this to you," Linda said. The other women in the room nodded in agreement.

Abby leaned the picture against the arm of the couch and hugged me again. "Thank you so much."

"That's it, everybody. Santa's bag is empty," Luke announced.

"Hang on. You missed one." Chase pointed to the opposite side of the tree from where Luke stood. Luke bent down to spy out the package, then jogged around to retrieve it.

"It's for Sally from Grandpa." He proudly handed it to me.

I'd already received so many wonderful gifts. All adult eyes were once again riveted on me. Thankfully, most of the kids had returned to playing with their new toys.

My stomach tensed and my hands grew sweaty at being the center of attention. I much preferred being behind the scenes. I ripped off the wrapping and opened the box.

Now it was my turn to say, "I don't understand." I gazed at Chase. "These are Sandy's reins."

"That's right. If I'd bought you a car, I'd be handing you the keys. I couldn't very well put Sandy under the tree, so I'm handing you her *keys*."

"Pop!" Was that a word of protest or surprise jumping out of Four's mouth? He managed the horses on the ranch, and Sandy was their best horse. "What a brilliant idea."

I sat dumbfounded. Finally I choked out "Chase," then swallowed hard, my gaze locked on him.

"Mommy, I'm hungry," little Heather whimpered.

Saved by a whimper. I didn't care. Any diversion would have suited me. I battled about accepting the gift, but it would be rude not to. Still, their best horse...and Chase was giving her to me? Why would he do that?

"*Now* Santa's bag is empty," Chase hollered. "Let's get these kiddos some peanut butter and jelly sandwiches to tide them over until the prime rib and ham are ready."

Chase's announcement successfully broke everyone's attention away from me. I fell back into the couch and let out a long breath. Mothers

190

herded their kids to the kitchen. Fathers cleared the floor of toys, placing them back under the tree, and crammed wayward bits of wrapping paper into the nearest plastic trash bag. Only Cohen, Hannah, and Chase remained by the time I gained the strength to stand. "I'll take these out to the barn."

"I'll join you." Chase fell in step beside me. "There's some paperwork that goes along with your *car*."

I waited until we were halfway to the barn before I spoke my protest. "Chase, I don't mean to be rude, but I can't accept Sandy. She's your best horse. Part of your breeding program."

"And she still can be. Just means we pay you for her foals." Chase stepped in front of me and stopped. "If ever a horse belonged to someone, that horse belongs to you."

The physical tension between us caused my stomach to flip-flop.

"I...I...thank you. A thousand times thank you."

Chapter Twenty-Six

CHASE

"There are three things that amaze me…how a
man loves a woman." Proverbs 30:18a,19d

I expected Sally would protest accepting Sandy, but maybe she felt too uncomfortable doing so in front of the whole family. My decision to join her on her trip to the barn was to give her that opportunity.

Now after hearing her thank you, I stood speechless and gaping at her. I discerned an openness in her I'd never noticed before. Snow fell all around us. With the ambiance of the snow, this seemed like an ideal first-kiss moment. But we stood in the middle of the yard where anyone could observe us. Why did this kiss pose such a problem to me?

"I'll sign Sandy's papers over to you in the next couple days. Her care will be up to you now, but I'll teach you what you need to know." I glanced up at the house. Michael and Four stood on the patio, gawking at us. Fortunately Sally faced away from them. I imagine her face would have turned beet red if she'd seen the funny faces they were making at me.

"Okay, I'll need that for sure. But are we going to keep just standing here? It's cold."

"Sorry." Neither of us had put on a coat before coming outside. I stepped aside for her to pass. "I, uh, I need to go start the prime rib."

Sally continued to the barn and I returned to the house.

"Good grief, Pop, I thought sure you were gonna kiss her." Michael snickered.

I crossed my arms. "Don't you two have something better to do than spy on me?"

"Nope," they said in unison, looking as though they were suppressing a belly laugh.

"I love you too." I patted Michael's shoulder, then Four's, and stepped to the patio door. Their kids clambered out as I opened it.

"Daddy, Daddy, let's build a snowman!"

We had planned Christmas dinner for earlier than usual to allow Emily and Matt to catch their plane to San Francisco. They didn't stay for dessert. I kissed Emily's cheek and gave Matt a firm handshake, saw them out the front door, then returned to the table to enjoy dessert.

I had barely pulled my chair up to the table when Abby rose.

"Merry Christmas, everyone. It's been such a wonderful day. The joy of family is only second to the joy of knowing Jesus." She looked down at Cohen. Perspiration dotted his forehead. "I waited until now to make this announcement because I didn't want to steal Emily and Matt's thunder, but Cohen and I are engaged."

Twenty protests sought their way out of my mouth, but I clamped my lips tight. The grandkids had long since finished their meal and darted off to the great room to play. The chatter they might have brought the room now left it in silence. Abby peered at the shocked faces around the table.

"I didn't expect *this* response." She dropped into her chair like a deflated balloon.

I noted each face to determine the emotion washing through them. Wide eyes, open mouths, a hand on heart, a hand across the mouth, raised eyebrows, and more. My family displayed the gamut of emotion.

"Abby, that's wonderful. It's just such a surprise!" Leslie jumped up from her chair and rushed to hug Abby, dispelling the heavy atmosphere. Once the initial shock wore off, words of congratulations went around the table and others offered hugs to Abby and handshakes to Cohen.

"Does that mean you'll be moving to Scottsbluff?" Sally's voice wavered. Her face lost its color.

Sally seemed to have some reservations about Cohen, yet she had encouraged Abby and Cohen's relationship. Why? And now that things had panned out, what questions raced through her head besides the one she voiced?

"We haven't thought that far. Cohen only proposed yesterday while we danced at the reception. It won't be a year-long engagement, but neither will it be an exceptionally short one."

Sally rose, walked to Abby, and hugged her shoulders. "I'm so happy for you." The color returned to her face. She released Abby and turned, pointing to Cohen. "You'd better take good care of her or you'll have me to deal with."

Cohen's eyes grew wide and his mouth dropped open. "I-I, of course I will."

If Sally wanted to keep Abby in Great Falls, threatening Cohen was the wrong tack. But maybe she was merely kidding. I couldn't be sure, and I don't think she was either.

Chapter Twenty-Seven

SALLY

"I prayed to the Lord, and he answered me." Psalm 34:4a

I couldn't help it. Another scene from the movie *White Christmas* invaded my thoughts. The fake engagement between Danny Kaye and Vera-Ellen. They thought it would encourage Bing Crosby and Rosemary Clooney to take the plunge. Had Abby and Cohen concocted the same thing? Surely not. Definitely not. Only I was crazy enough to concoct such a thought.

Chase was his own man. He couldn't be influenced that way. Or were they trying to push me toward the idea? It was ridiculous to think they would, or that they would even try. But think it I did.

Being closer to Abby was a large part of why I decided to move to Great Falls. Now that sat in question, but I couldn't voice my grief at the thought. I hated it when people deliberately said things to me to make me feel guilty about a decision I made. I wasn't going to do that to Abby.

When dessert finished, I helped clear the table and wash the overflow of dishes that didn't fit into the dishwasher. Linda, Michael's wife Hannah—how would we distinguish between Michael's Hannah and Cohen's Hannah?—and Leslie plied Abby with questions as they divvied up the leftovers. That left me to my thoughts.

Did weddings always put single people in mind of the same for themselves? Abby and Cohen's relationship was nothing short of whirlwind. I laughed at that.

"What's so funny, Sally?" Hannah asked.

"What?" I looked up from the dish I was washing.

"You were laughing. What about?"

I rinsed the plate and put it in the dish rack to dry. "I was thinking that Abby and Cohen had a whirlwind relationship, and then it struck me that essentially a whirlwind, the blizzard, brought them together."

Abby nodded and laughed along with the others, then her face sobered. "Are you upset about our engagement, Sally?"

"No. But it happened so fast. I don't want to see you get hurt, that's all." I shrugged.

"If I do, I do. I'll heal."

"Wow, Abby," Linda exclaimed, "what an amazing calm you have about that."

"Yeah, really. Wish I could be that nonchalant about heartbreak." Leslie looked close to tears. Her marriage sat in ruins. How deep was her heartbreak? It hadn't been visible all day.

"Oh, Leslie." Abby caught her up in a hug. "It'll be okay if you keep the right attitude. Look for lessons to learn from the experience and don't allow yourself to wallow in sadness."

Abby held Leslie tight while the rest of us continued our jobs in silence.

"Mommy, mommy," Heather yelled entering the kitchen. "Come play games!"

She pushed at Linda's leg, endeavoring to move her. The happy clamor dispelled the heavy emotion that hung in the kitchen. We quickly finished our chores and joined the others at the dining room table for games.

But Abby's words the night of her first date with Cohen trotted through my head. *Every relationship carries the risk of heartbreak. You can't have a relationship otherwise.*

I had entered that territory with Chase.

The next day dawned routinely with Chase, Gabe, and Pete tending to the daily demands and chores of running a ranch. The morning passed quietly. Almost anything would seem quiet after the presence of twenty-some people and the screams and squeals of the grandkids having fun with their new Christmas toys. I'd never experienced such a Christmas and quite liked it.

At eleven o' clock I stood staring out the patio door, sipping contentedly on a cup of coffee while marveling at the snow village the kids built yesterday. A good twelve inches of snow blanketed the ground. That probably contributed to the lack of white noise in the air. Today, the sky boasted its Montana-blue expanse, and the sun glittered on snowmen, snowwomen, and snowbabies.

I heard the front door open and close and made my way to the foyer to see who it was.

"Abby, I hoped that was you coming in the door. Do you and Cohen have plans for today?"

"Nothing special. Why?"

"I'd like to show you the pictures I found of our biological father."

"Okay. Let me find Cohen and Hannah. Has anyone had lunch yet?"

"No, it's too early for lunch."

"Not when you skipped breakfast." Abby put her hand over her stomach.

I laughed. "Or when you have breakfast at five in the morning. ...I think Hannah's out in the barn with Gabe and Pete, drooling over the horses. Maybe Cohen's out there too." I shooed Abby toward the back door. "I'll pull out the leftovers."

In short order, we were all enjoying lunch and remarking on the grandkids ingenuity with yesterday's snowfall. Afterwards, the majority returned to the barn while Abby, Cohen, and I went to the great room.

I opened a file folder of printouts I pulled from the Internet and laid several across the coffee table. "They aren't as clear as I'd like them to be, but maybe I can contact the newspaper in Scottsbluff to see if they still have the negatives."

Abby and Cohen each picked up a page and examined it.

"Sally," Cohen shook his head, his brow furrowed, "this could be Mark! He wears a bucket hat just like that, only his doesn't sport the fishing flies."

"That's where I've seen that hat! On the coat rack in Mark's office."

"The resemblance is uncanny." Cohen tossed his page on the table and crossed his arms. "I could pull out twenty or more pictures from his family photo albums and you wouldn't know the difference."

Abby sat between us and flung her arms across our chests as if to keep us from bolting off the couch. "Sally, do you think…"

I looked at her with eyebrows raised. "Think what?"

"Maybe Mark is Robert."

I sat stunned. If true, it made the events of the last few months even more miraculous. "Abby, that's brilliant!"

Abby dropped her arms to her lap. "Cohen, what do you think?"

"I don't know. He's never mentioned being adopted. How would I even broach the subject with him?"

"Just pick up the phone and call him," I insisted.

"No, Sally." Abby's voice sounded deeper than I'd ever heard it. "Take it from me. This is a conversation you want to have in person."

"Oh, yeah. I wasn't exactly thrilled when I first spotted your picture on the dining room wall." I stood and paced the room, thinking of our next step.

"Pacing isn't going to get you anywhere," Cohen said.

"I'm thinking!" I glared at Cohen. "I'll need to make a return trip to Scottsbluff. I can leave tomorrow."

"Mark's not home." Cohen shook his head as he spoke. "He and my sister always spend the holidays in Arizona with their son and their grandkids."

"Drat. More waiting." I huffed. "Cohen, do you know if he's ever done a DNA test?"

"I have no idea."

"Argh!" I tilted my head back and growled. "This is so frustrating."

"Yes, waiting can be." Abby pursed her lips. "And I imagine the Marines are used to charging in."

I stuck my chin out. "No, we scope out the situation first and wait for the right time to *charge* in. But when a decision is made, we move forward, usually by first making a plan. Every turn I make it seems like an obstacle jumps out at me."

"This isn't an obstacle. It's a huge step forward. It just comes with some waiting time." Abby rose from the couch and walked over to me. "Look, I know how upset I was to find out at the age of fifty-eight that I was adopted. We can't dump this on Mark over a phone conversation." She turned to Cohen. "When do they get back from Arizona?"

"The second or third of January. I'm not sure which."

"So there you have it, Sally. You can go back to Scottsbluff on the fourth. What plans have you made for moving here?"

I looked at Abby, my mind a blank, then started gathering up the printouts and putting them back in the folder. "I've looked at a few houses, but Leslie's real estate agent isn't even willing to work with me until after the assault case against me is settled."

"Let's sit down and put together a plan. It's silly to continue to pay rent on an apartment you're not living in. You could rent a place in Great Falls or put your stuff in storage until you find a house. Either way, you can be moving forward with those things while you wait on your DNA test and for Mark to get back from Arizona."

"Abby, I'm amazed at how level-headed you always are." I took a deep breath and resumed my seat on the couch. "Let's get started."

Once my moving plans were made, I wanted to head back to Kansas City immediately to start packing. But I promised to spend New Year's with the Reynolds family, and I wouldn't break it. I spent the days leading up to New Year's Eve researching and hiring a moving company. I put them in direct contact with Jen so she could let them into the apartment to take stock of what packing needed to be done and how big a truck it required. Then I started calling storage facilities in Great Falls to find available space.

The magnetic tension between Chase and me hadn't eased. Instead, it seemed to have increased. I didn't know whether to broach the subject with him or not. I worked hard to act normal when around him every day. Each afternoon, he spent time teaching me how to physically care for Sandy. He explained all the body parts and what to look for like bug bites and scrapes. How to groom her, what to feed her, when to bath her. Certainly, a lot more upkeep than a car.

I breathed a sigh of relief when I learned New Year's Eve would be a quiet night of card games with corned beef and cabbage for dinner. In other words, no party with lots of people I didn't know, and better yet, no chance of dancing with Chase and kissing at midnight. Abby, Cohen, and Hannah attended a party in town at a popular restaurant. That left me, Chase, Gabe, and Pete at home.

"This isn't how we usually spend New Year's Eve, but with all the hoopla of Emily's wedding, I opted for a quiet evening this year." Chase cut into his corned beef.

"I don't typically do anything special beyond staying up till midnight," I said.

"So, you're headed home on the third?"

"Yes, as long as the weather is good. It'll be a ten-hour drive to Scottsbluff. I've already arranged to meet with Mark on the fourth. Please pray he's open to what I have to tell him and that he's willing to do a DNA test. I'll head for Kansas City on the fifth."

"It'll sure seem strange with you not here," Pete said. "I'll look after Sandy for you while you're gone. Do you know when you'll be back?"

"The moving company loads me up on the tenth. It'll take them three days to get here, but I should be back by the twelfth...if I don't run into anymore blizzards."

Chapter Twenty-Eight
SALLY

"Taste and see that the LORD is good. Oh, the joys
of those who take refuge in him!" Psalm 34:8

For the full ten-plus hours of drive time to Scottsbluff, I sought
the right words to say to Mark Brown about whether he was adopted. I prayed the Lord would give me the best words.

When I entered his office the next morning, warring butterflies
churned my stomach. "Happy New Year, Mark. I hope you had a great
time in Arizona with your family."

"Yes, we did, Sally, thank you. How can I help you today? I must say,
you certainly keep me busy."

"That thought occurred to me too. I even thought of putting you
on retainer." I chuckled and plunged forward. "This isn't lawyer-related
work. It's very personal and might be a bit upsetting, but I need you to
keep an open mind."

He sat forward in his chair and rested his elbows on his desk. "I'll
do my best."

"I don't know how else to say this…were you adopted?"

"Adopted? No. That's a very odd question to ask, and yes, very personal." He interlaced his fingers and I noticed his knuckles grow white.

I retrieved the folder of printouts I'd shown Abby and Cohen and
began to lay out the same pictures on Mark's desk. I started with the
one of the three of us at the orphanage. "This is a picture of Abby, me,

and our brother that was taken of us at the orphanage the day I was adopted."

A soft gasp escaped Mark's lips.

"These others are pictures of our biological father. When Cohen saw these, he said they were dead ringers for you."

Mark fell back in his chair, his mouth open. He cleared his throat then swallowed hard several times. His face flushed and it appeared he might be having a heart attack. I bolted out of my chair, adrenaline surging into my veins. "Mark, are you all right?"

He shook his head and waved me off. "I'm fine. Just shocked at the resemblance."

I took my seat again and a few breaths to slow my heart rate. "Then you understand why I asked if you were adopted. Are your parents still living?"

"Yes, they are, but they're nearing their nineties, and I'm not going to risk their health by asking them." He stood and paced the room.

I watched him for several seconds. "I grew up knowing I was adopted, but it was certainly a shock to discover I had a twin sister. And then we learned we had a brother. I can only imagine the shock it might have been had the state opened Robert's adoption records and you discovered it was you."

I watched his continued pacing. Was he merely thinking? Angry? Dumbfounded?

"Would you be willing to take a DNA test?"

His pacing jerked to a stop and he glared at me. "I don't know. Now, please leave, Miss Clark. I have to prepare for court."

I gathered my photos from his desk, shoved the folder into my purse, and left. I expected shock, but his demeanor bordered on controlled rage, his body stiff, his hands fisted at his sides, his jaw clenched. He had greeted me as Sally, but now it was Miss Clark. A distinct shift to formality.

What had been Abby's reaction when she learned she'd been adopted? Was she angry with her parents for not having told her? She'd had time to adjust to the idea by the time she and I met, and nothing in the past five months hinted at a reaction as strong as Mark's.

I texted Abby and Cohen with an update then hit the road for Kansas City. It was only 9:15 in the morning and waiting another day to drive home made no sense.

Abby, Cohen, and I were all convinced that Mark was indeed Robert. But if he refused a DNA test…would I be able to let it go? Would I be content to believe Mark was my brother whether he acknowledged it or not?

I stopped for the night in Lincoln, Nebraska, and finished the final three hours of the trip the next day. The apartment looked as though I'd never been gone. I called Jen and arranged to take her to dinner to thank her for looking after everything, then dove into clearing my closets and drawers of items I didn't want to move to Montana.

My first day back confirmed the wisdom of my decision to move. Traffic noise and the smell of exhaust assaulted my senses. An ice storm moved through that night and left me without power for a day. I mentally put *install a generator* on my to-do list for my new home. Even with all the tasks ahead of me, I already missed Abby, Chase, Gabe, and Pete. I hadn't realized how much a part of my day they had become. Did they miss me? Or were they relieved to have me gone?

The day before the packers were due, I boxed up my desktop computer and printer and loaded them into the trunk of my car. In all the moves I'd ever made, something always got "lost." My computer and printer were not going to be the casualties of this move. The packers arrived on the ninth and made quick work of boxing up my meager belongings. The moving truck arrived at 8:00 a.m. the next day. My excitement level grew as I watched them carry my furniture and boxes into the truck.

Tonight I'd stay at Jen's and tomorrow—barring ice storms and blizzards—I'd head back to Montana and a new chapter in my life. For the first time in my life, I imagined and believed a life as a successful writer, hitting the bestseller lists, and winning an award or two was possible.

In hindsight I recognized I had been making choices for my life all along that steered me in the direction I wanted to go rather than allowing others to make the decisions for me. I'd first done it as an eighteen-year-old when I stood facing jail time for my third offense at shoplifting. The judge offered the kid before me a choice of jail or the military, and I asked the judge why I couldn't have the same choice. I'd done it again when I applied for a transfer to embassy duty while in the Corps. And most recently when I quit my job at Pendrake Publishing and flew to Montana to claim my inheritance.

What did I want this new direction in my life to include? More to the point, *who* did I want it to include?

Chapter Twenty-Nine
CHASE

"She brings him good, not harm, all the
days of her life." Proverbs 31:12

I missed Sally the moment she pulled out of the driveway. Would she get back to Kansas City and decide she'd made a huge mistake about moving to Great Falls? That seemed unlikely. She loved nature, and the city didn't offer that. From what I had learned about her, once she made a decision she followed through with it.

Whether she realized it or not, the Sally that had arrived here in August was not the Sally who just left the driveway. Once she finally let down her defensive posture, her true self began to shine through. The holidays proved her to be kind, generous, thoughtful, and fun.

Her absence created a big hole in my day. I missed her cheery good morning at breakfast each day, our afternoon horseback rides, her bubbling excitement about the novel she was writing. I tossed around the idea of buying an engagement ring, but then scoffed at myself. We'd had one date and one dance. No romantic relationship had been established between us. But we'd spent every day together for the past ten weeks. More time physically together than Abby and Cohen.

Cohen and his daughter left the day after Sally. I took the opportunity to talk to Abby about her engagement.

"Abby, are you sure about your engagement to Cohen? Isn't it a bit too soon? You told me you were just having dinner, not getting engaged." Maybe I was just looking for confirmation that thinking of marriage to Sally so soon wasn't ridiculous. But then again, I didn't need anyone's permission to do what I wanted.

"I said that back in October."

"And I said I'd remember it."

"All right, I know it seems fast, but it's not like we're hormonal teenagers. Being stranded together for three-and-a-half days gave me a lot of insight into who he is. And we've talked every day since."

"Do you want me to walk you down the aisle?"

She smiled. "No. I want to keep things low key. Just family, with Pastor officiating."

"After Emily's crowd, I'm all for small. Let me know if there's anything I can do." I kissed her cheek. "Now, I need to get out to the barn."

I loved Sally, but did she love me? I'd spotted desire in her eyes more than once. I knew her hasty departure outside after our dance at Emily's wedding reception wasn't due to being overheated. But would she take the risk and open herself to fully experience what we could have together? Receptiveness to that idea appeared for the first time on Christmas day. But in her absence would she erect that wall of protection again?

For me, January 12 didn't arrive fast enough. Sally texted her expected arrival time as six or seven. Surprisingly, I had several texts from her with updates on her moving progress. Granted, it was a group text to both Abby and me, but all the same, she could have simply sent it only to Abby.

I had Rita prepare Sally's favorites, beef stew and cherry pie, for supper. The Christmas Day snow all melted shortly after Sally left for Kansas City. Those twelve inches were more than we normally get all winter. The weather radar showed a cloudless sky graced the Great Plains and I prayed it would stay that way.

Abby arrived at 5:50 to join us for dinner, and we both took up vigil in the great room to watch for Sally.

"So, Abby, have you set a wedding date yet?"

"I'm thinking May or June. I want to do it outdoors in my backyard."

"Does that mean Cohen will be moving to Great Falls?"

"Yes, it does. He's thinking of renting out his house as an Airbnb during the months Hannah is away at school. But enough small talk, Chase. Where do you stand with Sally?"

"Nowhere…well, we're friends."

"Balderdash. The electricity between you two since Emily's wedding is enough to power Great Falls for a whole day."

"Don't be ridiculous." I got up and walked to the window, blindly staring out toward the tennis court.

"Okay, maybe not all of Great Falls, but it's enough to light this house for a month. Have you talked at all while she's been in Kansas City?"

"No. I wanted to call her but didn't."

"Why not?"

I heard the slam of a car door and spotted Sally's car in the drive. I headed to the front door, but Abby grabbed my arm as I passed her chair. She stood and glared at me.

"You love her; she loves you. Stop pussyfooting around."

"Sweet Abby." I pecked her cheek. "Are you hoping for a double wedding?"

"*That* is an excellent idea!" Abby rushed to the door to greet Sally.

I watched as they hugged like it had been years since they'd seen each other.

"Welcome home! Chase had Rita make your favorites for dinner. Let's get your stuff into the house so I can tell you all about my wedding plans."

In the days that followed, we settled into the routine we'd found before Christmas, with Sally spending her mornings writing and her afternoons with Gabe, Pete, and the horses. She viewed potential houses but had yet to find one that met her criteria, and waited impatiently for her DNA test results in the mail.

Two weeks after Sally's arrival back in Montana, a TV station out of Rapid City contacted her, Abby, and Cohen about doing an in-studio interview for their afternoon show. After some lengthy discussion and prayer, they agreed. Tomorrow, Steve would fly them down there.

I rose early to allow more quiet time with Lord before diving into the day's chores. I traipsed to my office and knelt to pray.

"Lord, why am I having such difficulty telling Sally how I feel about her?"

You're concerned about that protective wall of hers. But she has torn it down.

"So that's why I've sensed an openness in her that wasn't there before Christmas. Good to know. Do I need to tread slowly?"

Simply be patient. She is learning new ways of thinking and behaving.

My cell phone dinged with a text message. Why hadn't I thought to put it on silent while I prayed? I ignored it.

Sally needs you.

I rose, retrieved my phone from the desk, and checked my messages. A text from Sally read: *In standoff with skunk. What do I do?*

Was she serious? Yes, skunks visited the barn but mostly at night. They controlled the mice that sometimes got into the horse feed. As yet, sunrise was two hours away. Maybe she was serious.

Don't startle him. Where are you? I dashed from the office and grabbed my coat from the front closet.

At barn entrance.

I ran out the back door and toward the barn. I arrived in time to see the skunk trotting off.

"Stop right there," Sally hollered.

"Glad to see he decided to go home, no harm done."

"No harm done? You must be standing upwind. I think those little guys are cute, and I half don't mind their smell when I catch a whiff driving down the highway, but up close and personal…it's awful."

"You like the smell of a skunk?" I started laughing.

"Yes, I know, I'm weird. What am I going to do? We head to Rapid City tomorrow for the interview with the TV station. I can't subject people to this stink."

"We'll get you cleaned up and smelling pretty even if we have to pour a whole bottle of perfume over you." I approached her.

"Chase, no. Don't come any closer. I don't want this smell to get on you. When Rita gets here have her get me some clean clothes from my room and whatever stink removal concoction I need and I'll use the shower in the barn."

"I don't care if the stink gets on me." And then the perfect idea came to me. What better time for our first kiss. How could Sally second-guess the depth of my love if I was willing to kiss her in the midst of all that stink? "What a story this will make..." I started belly laughing, unable to finish my sentence.

"I'm glad you find this so hilarious. You won't when you're subject to the smell all day."

"Did you get any spray on your face? Are you itchy at all? Breathing okay?"

"Yeah, I'm fine. I turned away the minute he aimed his butt at me. I think most of the spray hit me across the back."

"Okay. Rita usually gets in by six, so I'm sure she's already here. I'll have her get you clean clothes and I'll root out the stuff we keep on hand for just such occasions. But first, there's something else I need to do." I walked toward her.

"Chase, stop! You're clothes are probably soaking up the scent just by being here."

"I told you I don't care." I gently clasped her face in my hands and locked my eyes on hers. "I love you, Sally Clark, and I have every intention of kissing you right now."

She put her hands to my chest as if to push me away, but as I leaned down, she grabbed my coat and pulled me to her. I didn't want our kiss to stop but knew the sooner Sally got showered the better.

"As I tried to say earlier, what a story this will make...that a skunk brought us together. Now off to the shower."

Chapter Thirty

SALLY

"The words you say will either acquit you
or condemn you." Matthew 12:37

After that amazing declaration and kiss from Chase, I stood frozen in place. I watched him walk to the ranch house with him glancing back at me now and then. Once I was sure my legs wouldn't collapse under me, I made my way to the shower in the barn, thankful I wouldn't have to carry this stink into the house.

I pulled off my boots, then stepped fully clothed into the shower, the water as hot as I could stand it. After several minutes I stripped off my clothes and dropped them at my feet. Thankfully, I hadn't been wearing the white Stetson cowboy hat Chase gave me. I heard a knock at the door.

"Who is it?" I hollered.

"It's Rita."

I peeked out from behind the shower curtain. "Come in."

The door opened slowly and Rita entered, clothes and a black trash bag in one hand and a bottle of "skunk soap" in the other. She laid my clothes on the sink counter and handed me the bottle. "Read the directions carefully. Put your soiled clothes in the trash bag until you can get them to the washer."

"Don't worry about that. I'm going to burn them."

"Probably the best option."

"Thanks for bringing me this. I hope you don't carry the stink back with you."

"It'll be fine. Breakfast is ready whenever you are. Chase is already regaling Pete and Gabe with stories of your skunk encounter." She giggled and left the room.

Did those stories include relating our first kiss? Doubtful. I imagined the teasing Chase's sons would give him if they learned it took a skunk for him to finally kiss me. He'd never hidden that desire, but why had he been so reluctant? As I soaped and scrubbed myself for the next hour, I turned that question over in my mind and realized my wall of protection had probably stopped him.

If only I'd realized sooner how my own choices kept people out of my life. Well, now that I did know, I'd make changes.

As I made my way to the house for breakfast, I wondered how I should act around Chase now. How would he act around me? I breathed a sigh of relief to find the dining room empty. I gulped down a cup of coffee to calm my nerves, then fixed a plate of pancakes and bacon, and considered the situation. I had to talk to Chase and find out how this changed our relationship. His declaration of love seemed one step short of a marriage proposal.

By the time I finished breakfast, Chase, Gabe, and Pete had gone into town and weren't expected to return until after lunch. But I didn't see him again until dinnertime and I could hardly ask him with Gabe and Pete sitting across the table from me.

"I'm not very hungry tonight, but Chase I'd like to talk to you after dinner. I'll be in the great room." I rose and left the room.

Thirty minutes later Chase joined me.

"That new skunk remedy works pretty good." He stoked the fire then turned and gazed at me. The bronze flecks in his eyes danced with the firelight. "If I didn't know you'd been sprayed this morning, I'd never know."

"That's good. I certainly wouldn't want to carry that smell on board your plane or into the TV studio."

"I think we've all been sprayed at one time or another in our lives.

When you have to do chores in the dark, it can be hard to avoid the skunks."

"You've been sprayed before?"

"Once, when I was when a little tyke." He took a seat on the smallest sofa in the room and patted the seat beside him for me to sit. "What did you want to talk about?"

I stood rooted by the fireplace. Of all the furniture choices in the room why did he have to sit on the loveseat? I glanced into the hallway for Gabe and Pete. I didn't want anyone overhearing the conversation.

"The boys are downstairs in the game room, and Rita's left for the night. Now come sit down."

I sighed and reluctantly took a seat facing him. "That kiss took our relationship into new territory, but I'm not sure what territory."

"I love you, and I assume by the passion in your kiss that you love me. Though, I admit, I did send you off to the shower before you had a chance to say anything. Where do you want this go?"

"I'm willing to explore things. I-I…what about your kids?"

"They've known for several months how I feel about you. Not that I told them, but I've made no attempt to hide my feelings. In fact, I even took some ribbing for not kissing you on Christmas day when we were headed to the barn."

"Did they assume I wanted kissed?"

Chase snickered. "Oh yeah. They all saw us during our dance at Emily's wedding reception. Nobody could miss the electricity between us that day, except maybe Emily and Matt because they never took their eyes off each other."

"What do we tell them?"

"They're smart kids. I'm pretty sure they'll figure it out when I kiss you good morning at the breakfast table."

My stomach flip-flopped at the thought.

I breathed a silent thank you to God that Chase didn't kiss me at the breakfast table the next morning. Nervous butterflies about today's live TV interview had already taken residence and stolen my appetite. I didn't need any added butterflies from Chase kissing me in front of Gabe and Pete.

So now here we were—Abby, Cohen, Hannah, and I—about to be guests on an afternoon show that aired regionally across South Dakota and parts of Wyoming, Nebraska, and a small southeast corner of Montana. Cohen and Hannah met us at the Rapid City airport and drove us to the TV studio. The four of us prayed this morning via virtual meeting, at the airport, and now as we sat in the green room.

I'd come prepared with the picture of Reverend Joshua Salem at the church's fiftieth anniversary that showed the stained-glass window and a screen shot from YouTube of Travers' first report that lacked the window.

"Lord, Your Word says 'when they bring you to the synagogues and magistrates and authorities, do not worry about how or what you should answer, or what you say. For the Holy Spirit will teach you in that very hour what you ought to say.' We don't know if we are facing a non-believing show host and audience, but You do. We trust You, Holy Spirit, to give us the right words in response to the host's questions. Calm our nerves. Let us be mighty witnesses of Your glory. In Jesus' name, amen," Abby prayed.

Nothing is more powerful than words straight from the Bible. We looked at each other as Abby finished her prayer. As one, we took a deep breath and let it out.

Lord, help me keep my tongue under control, I prayed silently.

"We're as ready as we'll ever be. Now trust God to fulfill His words," Abby said.

"And if we need it, I've got pictorial proof." I patted my pocket that contained the pic of Joshua.

Moments later a runner summoned us to the stage, and a technician placed and tested a microphone on each of us.

"Hello. I'm your show host, Charles Kingman."

We introduced ourselves.

"First of all, relax. You're just having a conversation with me. Don't worry about the camera or where it's at. Just talk to me."

He seemed pleasant enough and I relaxed a bit. Maybe this wouldn't be so bad after all. "I expected to see Elizabeth Travers. Will she not be here?"

"She'll join us a bit later. A couple of the first responders will also join us at the half-hour break. We have a full hour for our interview, but we'll cut for commercials every ten minutes, so try and keep your answers as concise as you can." He smiled then went to talk with the cameraman.

The tech seated us and left us to ourselves. "This is stacking up to be pretty interesting. Might even be some fireworks," I whispered to Abby and Cohen.

"I had no idea it was going to be an hour long!" Cohen wiped the sweat from his brow with his hand. He looked imploringly at Abby.

"Relax, Dad. God's watching over you, over all of us," Hannah comforted him.

Mr. Kingman took a seat on the stage and we ended our conversation. A minute later the show began.

"Good afternoon, South Dakota," Mr. Kingman opened the show. "We're here today with the four people stranded by the blizzard that hit our area last October. This is Abby Reynolds and Sally Clark from Great Falls, Montana, and Cohen Reed and his daughter Hannah from Scottsbluff, Nebraska." He motioned his hand toward each of us as he introduced us. "I've seen the interview you did with Elizabeth Travers, and frankly, I find this *miracle* hard to believe."

"Then why did you ask us on your show? To make us look like fools and yourself the man of the hour?" I blurted. Another skeptic as bad as Elizabeth Travers.

"Whoa, Miss Clark. I'm intrigued. You stayed warm and fed for three-and-a-half days in an abandoned, burned out church. And you even say you met the former pastor Joshua Salem."

"Yes, sir, that's what makes it a miracle, Mr. Kingman," Abby said.

"Miss Reynolds, you're from Montana. What took you to South Dakota?"

"My sister and I were headed to Mt. Rushmore when we got surprised by the blizzard."

"And what about you and your daughter, Mr. Reed?" he asked.

"I crashed into a ditch because I didn't see the curve in the road. We could barely see ten feet in front of us it was snowing so hard. Thankfully Hannah spotted the church nearby."

"Me and Dad saw the burned part of the church, but Abby and Sally didn't see it that way at all. I watched Dad put his hand on the pot belly stove and not get burned, yet a minute later Sally poured him a cup of hot coffee that had brewed on that same stove. He touched it again and nearly burned his fingers." Hannah looked at her dad for confirmation of what she'd said.

"We don't know how things happened the way they did. That's what makes it a miracle." Cohen reached over and clasped Hannah's hand.

How were we going to get through an hour of this? We answered his questions as clearly as we could, but it appeared he was out to prove miracles didn't happen.

"We're going to cut for a commercial break, folks. When we come back, our newest reporter, Elizabeth Travers, will join us."

Elizabeth stepped out from behind the camera and up onto the stage, a Cheshire cat smile pasted across her face. She sat in the empty seat next to Mr. Kingman's.

It appeared we were going from the frying pan into the fire. Papa, let the truth be known. We dared not say anything to each other, but the four of us exchanged glances. Hannah and Abby looked confident. Cohen, nervous, like myself.

You prayed for me to give you the right words. Do you not trust me to answer?

God's words hit me between the eyes. Papa, I'm so sorry. Forgive me. I closed my eyes and focused on God.

"Welcome back to *Good Afternoon, South Dakota*. Joining me is Elizabeth Travers, who first brought us this story back in October." Kingman turned to face Travers. "Elizabeth, I understand you've been to this church. What did you find?"

"A burned out shell. It's a wonder the wind hasn't blown it down. These people could not have stayed warm or fed while there."

"And what of the pastor, Joshua Salem?" Kingman asked Travers.

"Joshua Salem founded and pastored Christ Community Church for fifty years. He died in 1992." Travers directed her answer to Kingman, then turned and looked at us. "Why do you insist on perpetrating such a hoax?"

"What did God do that you hate Him so vehemently, Ms. Travers?" Hannah asked. This jerked Travers up short.

"We're asking the questions here, not you. You put every first responder at risk with your stunt. You should be brought up on criminal charges."

Her response didn't stop Cohen from stepping into the fray. "Ms. Travers, was my crash into the ditch a stunt?"

"No."

"But yet you insist that moments after I crashed I decided to pretend to be stranded and got three other people to play along with me?"

Oos and ahs erupted from the show's live audience. Travers' face paled.

Now Kingman wore the Cheshire's smile. Had this been his plan all along? To make Travers look the fool? But why? He'd seen the first interview Travers did with Abby and Cohen. This rivaled Saturday Night Live humor and was less believable than our miracle.

"It was not a hoax," I insisted. "Haven't you interviewed the first responders? We fed the crew from the fire station breakfast before they left. Was that policeman who took Cohen's accident report not astounded by what he found? He knew the history of the church."

"Speaking of first responders, we have Chief Schmidt of the Edgemont Fire Department and Officer Charles Hanley from the Edgemont police waiting to join us. Let's bring them out," Kingman said.

The audience began to clap as the two men stepped up onto the stage and took the last two empty seats.

"Welcome, gentleman. Officer Hanley, what did you find when you got to the church?"

"A dilapidated building, but it was warm and they served me hot coffee."

"And you, Chief Schmidt?"

"Quite the opposite. Could of had Sunday service there except for the storm. Every pew had a plush red cushion. The place was as warm as this studio is. They served me and my four men a full breakfast of bacon, eggs, pancakes, and hot coffee. And I spoke to Reverend Salem as well. These folks were probably more comfortable than most because they had heat, a way to cook, and plenty of food and water."

"That is interesting," Kingman interjected. "Very different accounts indeed."

"If we had perpetrated such a hoax, wouldn't we have brought the story to the news instead of the other way around?" Hannah asked.

"What do you mean?" Mr. Kingman asked.

"We didn't tell anybody about what happened. She," Hannah pointed to Travers, "found my dad through the accident report. And hounded him until he agreed to an interview." Hannah sat tall.

I observed the look of panic on the show host's face. He had lost control of his interview and he knew it. Would he cut to an unplanned commercial to shut us up?

"Prove to me this wasn't a hoax," he demanded.

"Kingman, if this was a hoax, you're saying I was a part of it. Not on God's green earth would I put my men at such a risk." Sounded like Chief Schmidt had some history with news reporters.

I glanced at the camera then said a silent prayer for the right words and the calm to deliver them with conviction and not anger. "Mr. Kingman, Ms. Travers, you have made it more than obvious that no matter what we say or show you would be proof enough for you to believe us. However, we're not here to prove anything to anyone. And we don't *need* to prove ourselves. We are not in a court of law. If we were, it would be up to the prosecution to prove our guilt, not us proving our innocence. You are not our judge or jury. No hoax was perpetrated. We know what happened. We were there. We could present irrefutable proof, but in the end, what you choose to believe is beyond our control."

Someone from the live audience began to clap, then another, and another. Soon, nearly the whole studio audience was clapping and cheering, and Mr. Kingman and Ms. Travers sat speechless. Finally, Kingman raised his hands and motioned for the audience to stop clapping, even though the station prompter had been trying the same thing.

"You have irrefutable proof?" Travers finally squawked.

"Sally has pictures." Hannah's eyes lit up. "Proof positive."

"Pictures can be photoshopped," Travers objected.

"I have a photo from a 1992 newspaper article of the church's anniversary." I leaned a bit to side and pulled the picture from my pocket. "And a photo on my phone of Ms. Travers standing in the same spot as Rev. Salem stood in 1992."

I handed the picture to Mr. Kingman. While he examined it, I pulled up the other photo on my phone then handed it to him.

"What do these prove?" Mr. Kingman asked.

"Why don't you have your techs scan them and put them up on the screen so we can all see them?" Chief Schmidt suggested.

"Excellent idea, Chief." Kingman plastered on a smile, then turned toward the audience. "Folks, we'll cut to a commercial break while we prep the photos." He waited for the light atop the camera to go dark then turned and shot us an angry glare. "You should have brought this to us ahead of time."

"How were they to know they'd need it?" Chief Schmidt asked. Kingman ignored him as a makeup man dabbed at Kingman's sweaty face.

I leaned over toward Chief Schmidt. "Thanks for standing behind us, Chief."

"I wish I could say there was no selfish motive behind my actions, but the fact is, they're calling me a liar as much as they are you. I'm the person who told that fool reporter about the miracle in the first place. And you're right. They probably won't believe a true miracle occurred no matter what you show them."

"Quiet please," someone on the set hollered.

We all ceased our conversation and waited for the cameras to go live again.

"I'd like to apologize to our viewers for that unplanned break, but I think the next few minutes will be worth any confusion this has caused," Mr. Kingman announced. "Terry, you want to put up the picture of Reverend Salem?"

We waited for the picture to appear on the screen behind and off to the side of us.

"Can you explain what we're seeing, Miss Clark?" Mr. Kingman said.

"This is Reverend Salem standing at the pulpit during the fiftieth anniversary ceremony the church held. A newspaper out of Edgemont ran this article the same week as the ceremony. I want you to pay particular attention to the stained-glass window behind him." I fell silent and allowed Kingman and Travers and the studio audience to observe the picture.

"And why is that window important?" Mr. Kingman asked.

"Because it's there," Abby said, picking up the thread of the conversation. "Ms. Travers insisted there was no stained-glass window, despite what we told her during our interview with her in October." Abby nodded at me and I continued.

"If you'll put up the other picture from my phone you'll see Ms. Travers standing at the pulpit during her first TV report of the incident."

The picture flashed onto the screen and within seconds, gasps, oos, and ahs escaped from the studio audience. The lack of the window was clearly visible to them.

"I ask you, Mr. Kingman, did we perpetrate a hoax? Did Ms. Travers doctor the scene during her report to discredit us? Or did a true miracle occur?" I looked at Kingman, waiting for his answer. Travers' face had lost all color. Her body slumped in the chair, and she rapidly blinked as she stared at the photo.

"I, uh, I…" Travers attempted, then seemed to pull herself together. "I didn't doctor anything."

"Ms. Travers, when we got caught in that storm on the way to Rapid City, we prayed for God to provide us shelter," Abby said. "He did that and so much more, but then God often does. We were as surprised to learn of the church's history as you were. What we experienced was as if the church was as alive today as it was back in 1992."

"I'm sorry, folks, but we're out of time," Kingman interjected. "But thank you so much for being here with us today. Looks like we might have a miracle to add to history of the Ardmore record books."

We couldn't get out of the studio fast enough. A security man escorted us to our car, yelling at the live audience that now crowded the parking lot to let us through.

"Great interview!" someone hollered.

"Way to go!" another yelled.

We clambered into the car.

"Wow, who would have guessed the audience would agree with us and not the show's host?" Hannah got comfortable next to me in the back seat of Cohen's car.

"You did a great job, sweetheart." Cohen flashed her a big smile then started the car. "Where're we going for dinner?"

"We were on the region's most popular afternoon news show. Can we go anywhere and not be recognized?" I shook my head. I didn't want people constantly interrupting me while I ate dinner.

"We'll have to chance it," Abby said. "Besides, you've said you want to be a bestselling author, so you might as well get used to people recognizing you."

She had a point.

"How did it go, ladies?" Steve greeted us at the bottom of the steps leading up into the plane.

"Like being on trial, Steve. I can't believe that between what Chief Schmidt had to say and the pictures we showed them, that Mr. Kingman still only grudgingly said 'we *might* have a miracle.'" Abby took the five steps up into the plane.

I followed her, and Steve followed me then stepped to the left into the cockpit. "Think they'll stop asking for interviews?"

"That station won't want us back, but who knows who else saw it. We might get inundated in the coming days."

I hoped that any calls we got would be from places that actually believed miracles still happen. Hannah had taken a lot of pictures of our time at Christ Community before she got sick, and they showed an interesting progression of the condition of the church. But like Travers said, photos could be doctored, so in the end, it still boiled down to what one chose to believe.

The events of the past two days and nervousness about the interview caught up with me, and my energy level crashed. It was only 8:15, but we had an hour-and-a-half flight yet ahead and a half-hour drive home. I collapsed into a seat and so did Abby.

"Chase'll have tons of questions when we get home. I'm going to rest my eyes until then." Abby settled down into the cabin chair, tipped her head back, and closed her eyes.

I took a cue from her and did the same.

Chapter Thirty-One

CHASE

"Daniel, servant of the living God, has your
God, whom you constantly serve, been able to
deliver you from the lions?" Daniel 6:20c

I watched from my pickup truck as Steve taxied to our private hangar. The minute he shut down the engines, I got out of the truck. I approached the plane and waited for him to lower the stairs. "Thanks for taking care of my favorite ladies, Steve."

He tapped his right eyebrow in a two-finger salute to me, then stepped back to allow Sally and Abby to deplane. Sally appeared first.

"Way to go, you two. You all knocked it out of the park. I want to hear what happened during the commercial breaks."

"Egads, Chase. Let us at least deplane first." Sally stepped down to the tarmac, and I snatched a quick kiss. I wrapped my arm around her waist and pulled her close while we waited for Abby.

"It's about time, you two." Abby winked at me while she descended the stairs. "Today has been the experience of a lifetime." Abby rolled her eyes and let out a groan.

I glanced at Sally. If she blushed at Abby's comment about us, I couldn't tell in the dark. "Based on your tone, sounds like things were rough."

"Like stepping into the lion's den—"

"But God shut that lion's mouth well and proper." Sally raised her hand as if she wanted to high-five Abby.

"Yes, He did. But I'm exhausted and it's late and I've got an important meeting tomorrow. Let's go home."

We piled into the front seat and I headed for Abby's house in Great Falls. "So do I have to wait until tomorrow to hear what didn't get broadcast?"

"Not much happened during commercials until after Chief Schmidt came on." Abby got comfortable then buckled her seat belt. Sally sat in the middle next to me. Had I not needed my right hand to shift gears, I would have put my arm around her.

"Go on." I started the truck, shifted into first, and pulled out onto the road toward the airport exit.

"You tell him, Sally. I saw you talking with the chief but I couldn't hear everything you said."

"I thanked him for standing behind us, but he said it wasn't all without selfish motive. He fully realized they were calling him a liar as well as us. He wanted to protect his rep and his men. The tension in the studio was palpable. Was it visible?"

"Yeah. Everyone looked tense, like a bow string ready to break."

Sally raised her hands in surrender. "I say Hannah wins the MVP award for the whole interview."

"Oh yeah? Why?" At the airport gate, I checked the traffic then turned onto the highway and headed for Abby's.

"When she asked Travers, 'What did God do that you hate Him so vehemently?'" Sally scoffed. "Left Travers with her mouth wide open for a few seconds."

"Plus she made a valid point about the fact that if we had perpetrated a hoax, we would have been the ones to notify the news, not the other way around," Abby added.

"I thought you four did a great job. You had more control over the interview than the host."

"I'd like to watch the interview on the TV station's webpage or YouTube. I want to see how we came across to the audience," Sally said.

We drove the rest of the way to Abby's in silence. I walked her to her door and waited for her to unlock and open it. "Good night, sis. Sleep well." I gave her a peck on the cheek, then waited until I heard the click of the lock and the clack of her shoes on the tiled entryway.

"So, you certainly put those reporters in their place," I told Sally when I settled myself back into the truck.

"I don't know about that. I think the strongest thing I had to say was that we didn't have to prove anything to anyone, and what he chose to believe was beyond our control."

"Well, it's over now so breathe easy. By the way, this came in the mail today." I grabbed the 9 x 12 manila envelope from the dash and handed it to Sally. "I thought you'd want to see it right away. It's from the DNA lab."

I stole glances at her as I maneuvered north on the city streets. "Are you going to open it or stare at it until we get home?"

"Probably stare at it. I can hardly read it in the dark."

I reached up and switched on the cab light. "Does that help?"

"A little." She sighed. "I guess I didn't think this through very well. Mark got so angry when I asked him about being adopted. I thought his reaction was way out of proportion. I thought this might get me the answers I needed, but now…"

"Now…what?"

"I discover possible relatives or I don't. Exciting or disappointing."

I heard the rustle of paper as she tore the envelope open and pulled out the documents it contained.

"Wow, there's a lot here to wade through. I think I'll leave it until we get to the ranch. I'll be able to see it better." She switched off the cab light and darkness swallowed us. "I don't know if I'll ever get used to how dark it is in the country."

"I got some other news in the mail today. Jake's trial has been canceled. He's decided to plead guilty."

"Chase, that's great news…well, not for Jake, I guess." She yawned. "How's Leslie doing?"

"Surprisingly well. She's quite a changed woman since you came here."

"I had nothing to do with that." She yawned again, long and hard.

"You helped her wake up to how far away from God she'd gotten."

227

"I think the adrenaline I've been running on has deserted me. I'm so tired all of a sudden."

"I would have thought the results of that DNA test would be enough to keep you awake. Only ten more minutes till home. Put your head on my shoulder if you want."

She scooted closer and did just that. When I pulled into the driveway, her soft snores filled the cab. I jiggled my shoulder to wake her up. "Sally, we're home."

"Hmmm? Oh, okay. Why can't I fall asleep that fast every night?" She scooted to the edge of the seat, and I helped her down, the DNA results clutched in her hand. "I'll look at these in the morning."

Chapter Thirty-Two

SALLY

"Those who look to him for help will be radiant with joy; no shadow of shame will darken their faces." Psalm 34:5

Sun rays peeking through the curtain woke me the next morning. That meant it was after eight o' clock already. Good thing I didn't need to be anywhere.

Giddiness prompted a smile I couldn't and didn't want to suppress. A deep sense of freedom swirled within me. Since Christmas day when I demolished my wall of protection, an openness and freedom had been growing within me. Today, I felt its physical presence like I'd never felt it before.

You shall know the truth, and the truth shall set you free.

I understood that Bible verse in an entirely new way. "Thank You, Papa," I whispered as I lay in bed. "Thank You that with You, all things are possible. For the first time in my life, I truly believe that. Forgive me, because my refusal to let things in also kept You out to a degree as well."

I threw back the covers and discovered I still had on the pants and shirt I'd worn for the interview. At least I had managed to take off my shoes before collapsing into bed last night. I sat up and looked around for the envelope from the DNA lab. I found it next to my shoes.

As I stared at the envelope, the faces of people I knew paraded through my mind.

Mrs. Randall and Sarah from my growing up years in Scottsbluff. My previous employer Mr. Pendrake and his wife in Kansas City. My friends Jen and John Maxwell.

God had placed families in my life all along the way, but I'd been too angry to see it. Too closed to receive and enjoy what they each brought to my life. Sadness for this loss briefly brought tears to my eyes. I'd write each of them a letter of thanks before day's end.

Now God had brought Abby and Chase and all his kids. Each loved me in their own special way, and I had grown to love them as well. I finally understood the inheritance God wanted me to embrace.

I stood and walked to the window to soak in the sunshine. And with it the light of God's love. I grabbed my Bible from the nearby table and turned to Isaiah 61:7, the verse that had begun this journey of inheritance. I read out loud, "Instead of shame and dishonor, you will enjoy a double share of honor. You will possess a double portion of prosperity in your land, and everlasting joy will be yours." I closed the book and put it back on the table.

If my relationship with Chase fell apart, it didn't matter. If I never had certainty about my brother, it didn't matter, though Mom had prayed we would find each other and I trusted God to answer. If I never learned more about my biological parents or if they'd left anything behind for us, it didn't matter. Because God had always been, was, and would be watching over me. For the very first time, the *everlasting joy* of His presence resided in my soul.

I retrieved the lab's envelope from the floor and pulled out the documents. I scanned long enough to find Mark's name listed as a familial match. I wondered how his DNA got into the system. But then maybe he'd had his owns doubts about his parentage and had been tested. Maybe he had been angry with me out of shame and guilt he felt for questioning his parents.

I sighed. I'd give him time to come around to the idea, then broach the subject later.

I changed clothes and went down to see what I could scrounge for breakfast.

"Good morning, Rita. Is there any breakfast left?"

"In the fridge. Help yourself." She loaded several bowls into the dishwasher. "Chase said to let you know he's got something for you. He's in his office."

"Okay, thanks." I pulled out the leftover scrambled eggs and slipped the dish into the microwave, then grabbed a slice of bread and put it in the toaster. "I'll go see him as soon as I eat breakfast. I can't believe I slept so late. I'm surprised Chase didn't wake me up. I've got chores to do."

"He said it was late when you got back from Rapid City. I watched the recording of you all during breakfast. It already has over 100,000 views and more comments than I had time to read. Mr. Kingman and Ms. Travers certainly have egg on their faces today."

"Holy cow! Guess I'd better read some of those comments so I know whether to expect more reporters on the doorstep." My toast popped up. I buttered it and visited a bit more with Rita while I ate, then walked to Chase's home office.

"Good morning, Chase. Rita said you have something for me."

He looked up from the work on his desk. "The rest of yesterday's mail for you." He grabbed a couple business-sized envelopes and held them out to me, then leaned back in his chair. "Your face is glowing this morning. Even more than when you came back from being stranded by the blizzard. What's up?"

"An amazing quiet time with God. He's brought me everlasting joy. I've never understood joy or experienced it like I did this morning." I looked at the letters Chase handed me. "These are from the courthouse." I ripped them open, pulled out the letters, and skimmed them.

"Can you share?"

"Jake dropped his case against me, and this one's about the trial, which you told me last night. I put these two things in God's hands and refused to think about them. And God answered amazingly." I smacked the letters against my hand. "That means the bank has nothing to quibble about in giving me loan. I'd better get my chores done. I'm going house shopping this afternoon."

Chase slowly rocked in his chair and twiddled with his pen. "About that. Why don't you stay here?"

"Because I need my own space. My room currently serves as my office, my prayer closet, my sunroom, and my bedroom."

"There're plenty of rooms in the house. We can convert them into whatever you need."

"And what do I do with the rest of my furniture?"

"I'm sure we can accommodate it."

I sighed. "I don't know, Chase. I'll think about it." I turned to leave.

"Sally, wait a minute." Chase rose from his chair and walked to where I stood in front of his desk. "Let me rephrase that."

He cupped my face in his hands and kissed me. "Stay here."

He kissed me again.

"As my wife."

He kissed me again. "How can—" and again, "I—" and again. I finally had to place my fingers over his lips long enough for me to answer. "How can I answer if you won't stop kissing me?"

"I thought my kisses might help convince you."

I smiled. "The first one accomplished that."

Author Bio

Debra L. Butterfield has been writing since she was a pre-teen. Her writing career began when she was forty-five years old and Focus on the Family hired her as a junior copywriter. She is the author of eleven books and has contributed stories to numerous anthologies and magazines. She blogs about writing at TheMotivationalEditor.com and is a freelance editor.

She is a US Marine Corps veteran, enjoys the outdoors and, oddly enough, likes the smell of skunks. Like most writers, she loves to read (cozy mysteries are her favorite), and usually not one book at a time either. She has lived as far west as Hawaii, as far east as Germany and lots of places in between. Now living in Missouri, Debra has three adult children and two grandchildren.

Claiming Her Inheritance

She just inherited a fortune... but the
strings attached could unravel everything.

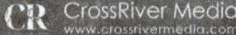

Sign up for the latest
updates from Debra

by scanning the QR code, and
receive her ebook *Mystery on
Maple Hill* for free.

Did you miss
Claiming Her Inheritance **and** *Discovering
Her Inheritance*, **books 1 and 2?**
Purchase your copies today at
CrossRiverMedia.com.